## "Piper, over here!

"See, there's Mom." Lance pumped the little girl's hand.

Instead of letting go, Maelyn squeezed his hand tighter. "Yay. Let's go tell her about the big bath for the apples."

Lance began to laugh but must've thought better of it when he noticed Piper's face.

She was as pale as the picket fence behind her, and instead of running up to her daughter, she was frozen except for her quivering chin.

When Piper furiously prayed that Maelyn would show up that very second, all the panic coursing through her veins must have caused her distraught brain to dream up this unbelievable scenario.

Maelyn held fast to Lance's hand, and there was no bashful tint on her cheeks or fear in her eyes. In fact, her little girl clung close to the secure hand, nearly pressing her cheek affectionately against the masculine arm…of her daddy.

Piper blinked several times. Nope, not her imagination. *This was happening.*

**Angie Dicken** credits her love of story to reading British literature during life as a military kid in Cambridgeshire, England. Now living in the American heartland, she blogs about author life along with her fellow Alley Cats on *The Writer's Alley* blog. Besides writing, she is a busy mom of four and works in adult ministry. Angie enjoys eclectic new restaurants, authentic conversation with friends and date nights with her Texas-native husband. Connect with her online at www.angiedicken.com.

### Books by Angie Dicken

### Love Inspired

*Once Upon a Farmhouse*
*His Sweet Surprise*

### Love Inspired Historical

*The Outlaw's Second Chance*

Visit the Author Profile page at LoveInspired.com.

# His Sweet Surprise

## Angie Dicken

### LOVE INSPIRED
INSPIRATIONAL ROMANCE

**LOVE INSPIRED®**
INSPIRATIONAL ROMANCE

ISBN-13: 978-1-335-58577-6

His Sweet Surprise

Copyright © 2023 by Angie Dicken

Love Inspired
22 Adelaide St. West, 41st Floor
Toronto, Ontario M5H 4E3, Canada
www.LoveInspired.com

Printed in U.S.A.

Intreat me not to leave thee, or to return from following after thee: for whither thou goest, I will go; and where thou lodgest, I will lodge: thy people shall be my people, and thy God my God.
—*Ruth* 1:16

To my sons. Thank you for the memories that inspire my writing more than you will ever know.

To my daughter. I am amazed by your love for life, friendship and creativity. You are so beautiful to me!

# Chapter One

Piper Gray threaded her short ponytail of red curls through the strap of her baseball cap, thrilled to be at the orchard again. It had been eight years since she'd visited her best friend's family. But this was more than her former home away from home and a place to crash after high school escapades. Oh, this family farm and orchard were so much more than that. The roots that grew here were strong and deep. She'd witnessed them, longed for her own roots to resemble such loyalty and love.

Her excitement dipped as she considered the fact that the Hudsons had no idea how close Piper was to those roots now. She had buried the truth so deep within her, and endured such a miserable time for so long, Piper had hardly reflected on the magnitude of her secret at all. Only since she'd accepted Sidney's offer for a fresh start at the orchard during an impromptu cider date with Sid and her mom had Piper faced the truth of all she'd kept hidden.

Today was not the day for her conscience to get the best of her, though. Today was the day for a divorcée to find steady ground and move forward, no matter what hid beneath the surface. Piper Gray was the newest seasonal employee of Hudson Orchard—the one place where she was sure to be safe and cared for. No questions asked.

Her phone vibrated in her pocket. She still had it on silent mode from last night. When she changed settings, she noticed an unopened text message from Sidney, time stamped at two this morning. Strange.

Heads up, friend. Lance showed up early as a surprise last night. Please don't let it discourage you. You all have been through so much since that summer.

Piper froze in front of the orchard's café door. The scent of fresh apple fritters suggested she bypass the employees' entrance and cut through the café. But her rolling stomach rejected the temptation. Before receiving that text, a temporary position here was exactly what Piper needed. Hudson hospitality, a chance to repair her estranged friendship with Sidney and solid footing to give her daughter Maelyn a secure fresh start.

But Lance was here? He wasn't supposed to arrive until after the season—once Piper had a chance to find a more permanent position. Piper would have never accepted this job if she'd known who she'd face each day.

She swiveled around. Her car was in plain sight. But the whitewashed house with that welcoming porch was a beacon from her past, coaxing her to stay a while. If she was going to stay in Rapid Falls, then running into Lance Hudson was inevitable. Those family roots weren't going away anytime soon…

Piper sucked in the sweet morning air, turned on her heel, then managed to scrape the last of her confidence from the reserves of Piper-the-Great—the teen she'd once been. She rushed past the hay bales lining the walkway and crammed her hands in the back pockets of her jeans.

With another deep breath, Piper opened the door to the metal building that housed the business office and the production area for packaging apples. She tapped on the office door.

Sidney singsonged, "Come in."

Just the sound of her best friend's voice soothed Piper's jumpy insides. After all, Sid's renewed friendship was an answered prayer from a year of leaning into God—finally. Piper was meant to be here. She pushed open the door.

Sidney was behind the desk with her usual bright smile and that twinkle in her sapphire eyes. She donned the same khaki baseball cap as Piper—with the Hudson *H* above the bill—her bobbed black hair tucked behind her ears, brushing against her jaw. "Hey, Piper! Can you believe—"

Lance appeared in Piper's peripheral. She hadn't expected to see him right away. "Oh, hey, there, Lance."

"Piper Gray, newest employee… I hear." He shifted from one foot to another. Lance had hardly changed. His broad shoulders filled up the corner of the office. His dark hair was short as always, just not short enough to stop the curls spiraling along his forehead. He held a khaki baseball cap in his hand. Piper noticed the tan line where a wedding ring should be. Heat flamed along her neck. She refocused on Sidney.

"I can't believe we are all together again," Sidney squealed, but concern tweaked her brow as her gaze landed on Piper. "He showed up last night while I was feeding the baby on the porch swing."

"Been a while since I've been back in Iowa." He

cleared his throat. "And it's been a few years since we've seen you around here, Piper."

Piper shoved away her last moments with Lance— the confusion and shame. She hadn't deserved a guy like Lance. Breaking things off had been for his own good. He just hadn't known it at the time. She couldn't go there now. Not after all that had happened. Memory lane was more like a treacherous ravine with too many pitfalls.

Piper admitted on a giant sigh, "I'd say it's been a lifetime." An uncomfortable pause buzzed through the room. And as usual, when things got uncomfortable, Piper turned on the humor. "Promise I'm not here to steal Sid away for late-night fishing at Gunter's pond." She winked and reminisced a time long before her summer fling with Lance—when he'd found the girls drenched as they'd walked home well past midnight. Piper added, "You were such a protective twin." She rolled her eyes—just like she used to, but this time, she offered an apologetic shrug.

"And now you are working…for us." Lance mirrored the eye roll but laughed. "I guess you are working *with* us, is more like it. Going to be an interesting season."

Piper shifted. "And you? Giving up Denver corporate life to package apples?" Her old sarcasm was fully awake, and she gently tapped his arm with a fist, like old times. "What a guy."

Lance narrowed his eyes and smirked, lifting his hand up to catch her punch like he used to, but Piper flinched a little and withdrew her hand. Her playfulness surprised her. She'd thought it had been squelched by the past years of being criticized.

Sidney rounded the desk between them and hooked her arm with her brother's. "I told you, Piper. Lance hopes to revive the grocery distribution of apples. We weren't expecting him to start up this season, though. He even moved back into his old room, too. Funny, I return from life as a military wife while Todd's overseas, and you all move back home, too." Her usual grin stretched just a little past normal, and she raised her brows. Sidney knew about Lance and Piper's short romance the summer after they'd graduated high school. She also knew that one reason Piper hesitated to take this job in the first place was that specific conflict of interest. But Sidney had convinced her Lance wasn't visiting until Christmas.

"I know, I know. I am morphing from exec in a high-rise back into my farm boy roots." Lance crammed the hat onto his head. "But if there is one thing you and I know, Piper, it's that this orchard offers a soft place to land when things get tough." He startled Piper with a compassionate grin, not far from those she'd begun to fall in love with their senior year. On a stuttered sigh, he continued, "There's lots of work to be done, anyway. Can't believe the additional attractions you've added to the place, Sidney. No wonder Dad considered letting go of the grocery distribution. It's nearly an amusement park out here." His dimple appeared with a half smile, half sneer.

"Good thing you are up for the challenge of growing the production side of things, Lance. I can't help but focus more and more on all the fun. Even you will fall in love with the newest attraction of all." Sidney shuffled through the papers on the desk and pulled out a map of the place. "Look!" She pointed to a circled area. "A pumpkin patch!"

"Hey, I dreamed of a planting a pumpkin patch for

years." Lance snatched the paper from her. "You all never wanted to expand that way."

"I guess it's good you are back, then." Sidney crossed over to Piper. "Now that we have some extra hands, you can help make your dream come true."

Piper's best friend and her best friend's twin brother were the same as they had always been. Larger than life and ready to tackle truly great things. Piper definitely didn't want to revert to the kind of girl she was back then—needy, clingy, and finding whatever it took to have fun because Mom's then-husband was flat-out mean.

While Piper's ex, Garrett, hadn't been mean at first, he had always been controlling. She had truly been trapped. If the Hudsons had had any idea what Piper had been through in her marriage, it would suck out all the joy of this small office space. Sidney tried keeping in touch as best as she could during her husband's out-of-state assignments, but Piper didn't always have a phone to communicate with. All that was behind her. Now, she'd revitalize her zest for life in her very favorite place of all.

"Okay, Piper, you are officially on orientation." Sidney handed her a punch card and signaled for her to exit the office. "The machine is old, but it still works fine." Piper led the way out of the office, catching a whiff of Lance's cedar cologne as she turned away.

What had she gotten herself into?

"See here?" Sidney tapped the top of the machine on the wall above a long counter. "Just stick your card in there and it will punch the time. Same after you're done with work. Easy as pie."

Piper reached over with the card, but it flipped out of her hand and landed on the ground at Lance's boots. She bent to pick it up and so did Lance. They knocked heads.

"Ouch!" they said simultaneously and stumbled away from each other.

"Are you all okay?" Sidney's voice was thick with concern, but her tightly pressed lips and amused eyes gave away that she might burst with laughter.

"Hey, your newest employees are already in need of worker's comp," Lance complained playfully.

"Yeah, this is not what I signed up for." Piper swiped off her crooked hat and readjusted her ponytail before putting her hat on again. Her gaze crashed into Lance's, sending her heart into a choppy rhythm. His blue eyes shone with a spirited intensity she had forgotten over the years. She hadn't seen this look much when Lance was policing Sidney's every move during their mischievous days of pranks and midnight swims, but as they'd gotten older, Piper would catch this particular look at the most mundane moments—either while watching television or while helping Mrs. Hudson make pies. Soon, her biggest secret was a crush on her best friend's brother. But that July Fourth weekend after graduation, Piper had finally refused to look away anymore. She fell into his gaze—much more intriguing than lights in the sky. Lance Hudson had a way of setting off fireworks without so much as a spark of fire, but oh, those were different kinds of sparks, that was for sure. The rest of July was a bittersweet romance—knowing they were being reckless with their hearts since Lance was moving off to college.

Ugh, Piper was so over her reckless days. If she'd learned anything these past several years, it was the severe consequences of whims and trusting someone with her heart. She would not get wrapped up in any situation that called for trust again. Too much was at stake now.

She accentuated her internal pep talk with an audible

sigh and gave a reassuring thumbs-up to Sidney. "No worries, I am a-okay. No worker's comp…this time." She winked then held out a hand in caution at Lance. She jested, "I'm going to pick it up, okay, Lance? You just hold your horses."

"Be my guest." He smirked and stepped back. Piper was more than a guest here. Just being with the Hudson twins made her feel…at home.

After Piper clocked in, they walked out back through an open garage door. On the way, Sidney explained how the tornado last year had taken out the old storage barn where they'd stored a bunch of old equipment. While she explained that Grandpa Jo's turn-of-the-century pieces were ruined, Piper couldn't help but consider she had kept something from those Hudsons they knew nothing about—her greatest possession was her only joy in life, and the reason she finally found the courage to leave Garrett.

Piper trailed behind the siblings as they approached a work truck. The warm fuzzy feeling evoked by the twins' entertaining banter cooled as a shiver trailed down Piper's spine. She considered that her daughter Maelyn pretty much had the same warming effect on Piper as Sidney and Lance.

No wonder.

Maelyn was as much a part of the Hudson family as Piper's own. She was Lance's daughter, and he had no idea she existed.

Lance slid behind the steering wheel of the old Ford pickup he'd helped Dad pick out the first summer he'd been home from college. Sidney scooted to the middle of the seat, then Piper hopped in and shut the passenger door. Lance checked the rearview mirror and noticed his own jaw flinching. He feigned a yawn to relax but couldn't help but glance at Piper. After so many years, he expected vague familiarity. Nope. This was like a time warp where he played older brother to his twin—technically, he was two minutes younger than Sid—and kept an eye on that feisty best friend with the greenest eyes he'd ever seen. As they turned onto the dirt road that undulated through the property, he forced himself to ignore the more recent memories of Piper—his sister's best friend turned into Lance's first love—making his first months away at college miserable.

"Wow, I love the cutouts of the nursery rhyme characters." Piper craned her neck as they passed Jack and Jill along a hillside.

"We put those in two seasons ago. Dad was kind to let me work remotely. People love having photo ops with all the fall color in the background." Sidney pointed over the dashboard at the three little pigs' cutouts prancing up to a storage shed. "You really should bring Maelyn out here, Piper. She would love it." Piper nodded then giggled when the big bad wolf appeared after they passed the building. Sidney continued, "I can't believe you haven't brought her yet. Like, ever." She stuck her bottom lip out in her typical pout that initiated Lance's eye roll.

"I know. But you were off exploring the military bases of the USA, as every good officer's wife should." Piper flashed her brightest smile. Lance ignored the ancient tug in his chest. Seemed ancient, anyway. Even if it had only been eight years.

Sidney narrowed her eyes. "All those times I let you know I was visiting home, though? Waterloo is not far, and now you're living with your mom in Rapid Falls."

"I know. Been rough, Sid. That's all." Piper's voice

was quiet and low. Maybe slightly unsteady. She placed her hands on her knees. Knuckles white. No ring, although she'd married her high school boyfriend quickly after Lance had left for college. Lance looked away, trying to quell his curiosity about her situation. He hadn't come here to step back into his old high school Converse sneakers. Lance and Piper had a complicated past in common, but now, they were mostly coworkers. That was it.

"I'm sorry." Sidney placed her hand on Piper's. "So glad that this worked out, though. I've been pretty isolated with Todd overseas since May, and only Mom, Dad and baby Amelia to keep me company." She leaned into Lance. "And now you're here, too. Seems like Christmas to me." Sidney laughed, but when Lance looked over, her cheeks were flushed. He knew that look. She was embarrassed. Sidney was fully aware Lance's career change was the good to come from a difficult year. And Piper had mentioned life being rough for her, too. He didn't know anything about Piper's circumstance, but his own heart had been like corn husks trampled on a corn maze floor. To see his ex-wife's engagement announcement a few months after the divorce was finalized? At least now his passion was revived with good ol' Hudson ambition.

"I am glad to be here." Lance cracked his knuckles against the steering wheel. "And will be relieved once I give the ring back to Nonny—"

"What?" Sidney turned to him with her back to Piper, distress wrinkling her brow. "You'll remarry one day."

"Not any time soon. I'd rather build a rollercoaster in the middle of the pumpkin patch than depend on one more person."

"Interesting. I kinda feel the same way." Piper leaned

onto her knees and smiled at him. "Divorced and independent. Sounds like we've both grown in the same direction."

He sighed audibly, surprised at the solidarity in this unexpected reunion.

Sidney pressed back on the seat and placed one hand on Lance's knee and the other on Piper's.

His sister was sandwiched between two people who seemed to have landed here after hard times.

But she always had a way of finding the very best out of any situation. Even with her husband deployed, she maintained a copious amount of optimism. Lance wished he'd inherited some of that, but she must have gotten more than her fair share in the womb, he guessed. Because most days, Lance struggled to focus on the bright side of things. Yet, the orchard was a very tangible sun for him. He might not be able to muster up joy within, but he could sure take in the light of this place.

Sidney peered past him as the first row of the orchard appeared to the left of the truck. "Dad was itching to see you this morning, sleepyhead."

Piper cleared her throat. "Oh, you haven't seen him yet? Maybe I should have stayed behind. This seems like a family affair—"

"What?" Sidney exclaimed. "Piper Elaine Gray. You stop that. He's probably going to be just as excited to see you. Sorry, Lance. But Piper has been sorely missed." Sidney nudged him with an elbow.

Lance couldn't help but blurt, "Hey, who's the Hudson here?" He was certainly feeling that old vibe of brotherly annoyance. But when he caught Piper stiffen her back into the seat and scrunch her button nose, he redeemed himself with, "What I mean is, you don't have to state the obvious, Sidney." The corner of

Piper's mouth twitched as she turned to him with a glare, then an adorable wink. How had he forgotten Piper Gray all these years—when she'd once claimed every corner of his thoughts?

He parked the truck at the main gate to the orchard, just behind the entry booth, opened his door and escaped from his proximity to Piper and the times long gone by that she reminded him of.

Sidney jogged around and hooked arms with him. "I saw Dad at the third row of Juliets." She squealed and motioned for Piper to come closer, but she seemed just fine hanging back a bit.

The mature apple trees awakened in him an ambition that Lance hadn't experienced in quite some time. Boosting the grocery clientele for his family business was Lance's ultimate goal upon returning to Iowa. After having a buyer quickly snatch up his condo, and tying up loose ends at his office, he was thrilled to start his new position as soon as possible. By the look of these beautiful trees, Lance's job would be easy. And with every step upon the dappled grass, Lance welcomed the distance between this opportunity and the failure he'd wrestled with after signing those divorce papers.

Dad was ahead, halfway up a ladder, filling up a sack. As they approached, Sidney hollered, "Hello, up there!"

"Hey, Sid. Just getting a few samples for the café gift baskets." He stepped down the ladder carefully, not looking over at them. His hair was even more silver than last Christmas, and his arms were golden brown with a lingering tan. When Dad caught Lance's gaze with the same blue eyes as his own, the pent-up emotion from the past several months welled inside Lance's chest.

"Lance." Dad's voice cracked as he bulldozed toward him. "I didn't want to wake you this morning." Lance went in for a handshake, but Dad yanked him into a bear hug.

"I had no reason to stay in Denver. And what's that saying? No time like the present." Lance squeezed his eyes shut. The scent of Old Spice and coffee meant life was secure. Dad never once wavered in offering security to his family. Another reason Lance was okay with his career change.

Dad pulled away and patted his shoulder. "It's been a tough go, I know." Lance glanced back at Piper. She was several feet behind them, paying attention to her phone. "We've been praying for you."

He focused on his father. "Thanks, Dad. I guess the last to know is Nonny. I plan on telling her myself. One of the reasons I tried to get back so quickly."

"You're doing the right thing, telling her in person."

And giving her back the ring. Lance didn't feel right keeping it now that the papers were signed. He surveyed the rows of trees. "You all sure have done a lot with the place. Glad that fence is holding up." A few years ago, Lance and Dad had spent the summer taking down the rotten fence posts while his wife finished up grad school in Des Moines.

Lance lifted his hat, raked his hand over his hair, then pushed the hat down forcefully, frustrated that the memories of his marriage were tangled with this refuge.

"Sidney has been our visionary." Dad opened his arm to his daughter, who was dismantling the ladder. "All her creative energy went into making this an experience for families. This is the second season of our corn pool, slides and sack races. Pretty entertaining." His hearty laugh had the same calming effect as always.

Sidney called out, "Piper! Where are you going?"

They all turned their attention to Piper, who had weaved toward the You-Pick entry booth with her cell phone to her ear. She gave a quick glance and a wave but continued walking away.

Dad chuckled. "This is quite the kick-off to our season. Seems like a family reunion. Your mother was thrilled to see Piper a few days ago. She had been miffed the girl disappeared after high school. She'd treated her like a daughter."

Sidney piped in, "She hasn't told me much about her situation, but she has a daughter and is living at her mom's again." Sidney cast a wistful look ahead. "She was hard to keep up with. Didn't return my texts or calls most of the time."

"You are a good friend to give her a second chance, Sid." Dad and Sid grabbed the ladder together. Lance carried the bag of apples.

"Well, we were practically sisters," Sidney said. "Now, she's easing into a fresh start, trying to find stability for her little girl."

"Nothing like home for a fresh start." Dad straightened his shoulders. "She'd always referred to our house as her home away from home. Hope it feels the same for her now."

Lance placed the sack over his shoulder and squinted toward the booth. He could barely make out Piper's figure in the shadows. As they approached, she leaned on her elbows and pressed into the sunlight, peering out toward them. A slight frown pulled her mouth down only for a second. When Dad raised his arm and waved, her whole face brightened. Her invigorating smile shone brighter than the September sunshine.

"Hello, Don! I am ba-ack!"

And Piper Gray certainly was back.

Lance couldn't help but smile, too. He'd forgotten how exuberant his sister's best friend was. She certainly seemed like a reunited member of the family. Piper Gray's legacy around here was complex, but Lance was working to continue the Hudson legacy of apple growing. His recent bout with a failed marriage and the distant memory of first love wouldn't distract him. Even if the latter was the vibrant redhead, sharing this fresh start alongside him.

## *Chapter Two*

The rest of the day, Piper learned the different variety of apples and the pricing for the you-pick customers. Piper couldn't help but wonder about Lance while she followed Sidney around. He was in and out of her view all day. Heaving ladders across the place, dropping off boxes of sacks and baskets, setting up the freshly painted signs along the fence.

"Your brother is a busy bee." Piper turned and hopped up on the wooden counter that spanned the width of the booth, letting her legs dangle like her younger days sitting on the Hudsons' kitchen counter. "You sure you didn't know about his return?"

Sidney hooked a quizzical eyebrow. "And risk you running off for eight more years? Piper, I would never lie to you."

Piper knew that and flashed an assured smile. No need to explain her reason for keeping quiet all that time. Need-to-know basis was a good motto to keep moving forward. "So, how did he manage to have such a huge career change?"

Sidney finished up the chalkboard with the pricing list. "Dad has been wanting to retire, and since the you-pick operation is so profitable, he was going to end distributing to groceries. When Lance found out, since he's worked in commercial distribution, it seemed the perfect opportunity to finally leave Denver." Her voice lowered. "His ex is already engaged."

Piper groaned. "Why would she go and do that?"

Sid cocked her head. "She was having an affair. That's why."

Piper's face heated and she reached her hand out. "I'm sorry. I didn't mean to be callous. It's just… Marriage is not all it's cracked up to be."

"Well, it depends on the situation." Sidney gave a tight smile and tucked her hair behind her ears.

Ugh, this woman was caring for her infant while her husband was serving their country, and Piper had allowed her own garbage to surface. "I'm sorry, Sid. I am like the Granny Smith of your life—much too sour to take."

Sidney laughed at that. "I like Granny Smith apples. After some spice and sugar, they make excellent pies." She swung open the door and motioned to Piper with a flick of her head. "Come on, we'll walk back since it's so nice out. Mom's babysitting. Amelia should be done with her nap, and you can see her before you head home. She'll turn your sour into sweet." Piper knew that look on her best friend's face. Motherly love was the second most common ground they had. First was a childhood of memories together.

They stepped into the late afternoon sun. On the road ahead, Don drove the tractor pulling a trailer where Lance sat among hay bales. Sidney had mentioned that the hayride was the favorite way for families to go from the café and corn pool area to the orchard. The trailer was huge. The main stop was lined with long benches for guests to wait for their ride. Piper was slightly nervous for the crowd tomorrow. She hadn't been around crowds of people in a long time—only at school functions once Maelyn had started school. Most of Piper's engagement with folks outside of Garrett and his family consisted of the clerk at the nearby grocery, Maelyn's pediatrician and her dear neighbor, Sue. Her quick decision to keep her pregnancy a secret and avoid derailing Lance's college plans, had led to some of the hardest years of her life. No matter how the old times seemed so near with Sidney, and even Lance, around, Piper Gray was nothing like the spunky girl she had once been. Now, she was going to be the face of Hudson Orchard's You-Pick experience.

"Lance and Dad are driving that trailer a little faster than we will tomorrow." Sidney walked quickly. "Loads of kids make it a very careful jaunt."

The hayride turned down the lane, just past the cutout of the big bad wolf. That cynicism that crept into Piper's response about Lance's ex getting engaged bubbled up and soured her throat. Her spunk was certainly chased away, just like the three little pigs chased away that wolf.

Piper needed to get out of her head. "Does Lance have any kids?"

Sidney shook her head. "No. Amelia is the only grandkid. I'd love to get to know Maelyn. More than a quick 'hi' at your doorstep, I mean."

Piper offered a weak smile and the faintest nod, recalling the day that Sidney had surprised her by showing up to Piper's duplex, a few years ago. Garrett had been home sick, and Piper had been embarrassed by the messy house. The ladies had spoken for a few minutes on the porch, but Garrett had begun to grumble about the noise so Piper ended the conversation.

She took in the Iowa air and focused on the familiar homestead, rather than those bad memories.

When they got to the front, Piper stopped by the office to clock out then they headed to the house. She was happy that the decor hadn't changed—black-and-white-checkered curtains and framed rooster art with splashes of red and toile backgrounds. Home sweet home.

They crossed the well-loved hardwoods to the four seasons room. Janet Hudson sat in a white wicker armchair with a book in her lap and readers slipping down her nose. "Well, hi, there, working ladies." She put the book on a glass table and nodded to the baby swing in the corner. "She's been such a sweet girl."

"Thanks, Mom." Sidney scooped up Amelia. "Hello, chunky monkey." And the nickname was perfect. Amelia was as plump as any six-month-old could be. She rubbed her brown eyes with two dimpled fists, and her cheeks were full and flushed in the warm bright room. "Remember Auntie Piper?" Sidney turned around with the little bundle on her hip.

Piper tried to hook her finger in Amelia's little hand, but instead, the little girl reached out to her. "Ah, you are the sweetest." Piper pulled the baby to her own hip and kissed her soft head of black hair. Baby sham poo and a hint of milk. The scent warmed Piper. She loved babies so much, and her favorite memories were of snuggling with Maelyn as a baby.

Amelia cooed and grabbed at Piper's nose. Piper scrunched it, and Amelia giggled. Laughter filled the room, including a deeper, richer chuckle behind her. She looked over at the doorway.

Lance leaned against the doorframe with his arms crossed against his chest. "That little sound is the best in the world."

Sid scooped up a blanket that slid from the swing. "I recorded it a while ago and sent it to Todd. He says he listens to it every day."

Piper squeezed Amelia one more time and handed her back to Sidney, but Lance swooped in and took the baby, lifting her high and setting off a full-on belly laugh.

"Well, she sure does like her uncle," Piper exclaimed.

Sidney nodded enthusiastically. "They had a happy reunion at two this morning when Lance arrived. I hope she doesn't always expect to be entertained in the wee hours."

"Getting reacquainted with this teddy bear is important." Janet squeezed Lance's shoulder as she left the room.

"That nickname!" Sidney rolled her eyes. Piper refrained from doing the same, although she'd often teased Lance-the-teddy-bear when they were younger. "You want to stay for supper, Piper? Mom's cooking."

"Homemade macaroni and cheese," Janet called from the kitchen.

"Ah, no, thanks. I have to take…" Piper was distracted as she watched her daughter's father adore his niece. "Um, I have to take Maelyn to dinner. Mom is working late tonight." She fished her keys from her pocket. "You all savor every bite of that delicious dish."

"You know it," Sidney said, smacking her lips as Piper opened the side door to the wraparound porch. "Get some rest. Tomorrow is a big day."

"Definitely. See you all then." Piper jingled her keys in a casual wave—though there was nothing casual about the feelings coursing through her in that moment. She crossed from the private yard of the house, through the family vegetable patch and around the café to the parking lot, with her breath trapped in her lungs and her jaw clamped tight.

This was all so very awkward. Not what she'd expected. When Sidney had offered Piper the job, it had been after a tense discussion with Piper's mom—how she and Bill could help with Maelyn for a while, but Piper needed to contribute financially because they were pretty strapped. Money was an important factor, of course—Piper had never had much access to it in her marriage—but, mostly, this job was more about the chance to ease into the workforce. Piper had forgotten how tied she was to this place and these people. And those ties didn't break in her absence—they just frayed a little with life's wear and tear.

She couldn't shut off her brain, even with the windows down and the fresh country air whipping through her sedan. Seemed like Lance had his own struggles, but other than that, he hadn't changed much. She wished she could go back to the impression of him being an overbearing sibling to her friend and ignore the niggle of guilt that instantly sprouted at first sight of the teddy bear of a guy.

The man was not overbearing in the least. He was more like the courteous guy who'd sat beside her under a July Fourth Spectacular long ago. Kind and subtle but changing her life more than he ever knew. And the thing was, she couldn't regret any of it.

After wrestling with memories for the fifteen-minute drive to Mom's shady street, she let out an exasperated laugh. How could she regret anything? That one summer with Lance had brought her the little girl who was drawing with sidewalk chalk in Mom's driveway now.

Maelyn looked up, popped up off her knees and ran through the lawn to meet Piper as she parallel parked. "Mama! You're back!"

Piper hopped out and wrapped her arms around her daughter. "How was school?"

"It was good." Maelyn rested her chin on Piper's belt buckle, staring up with bright green eyes above a smattering of freckles, just like Piper's now-faded ones. Maelyn's two front teeth were missing, and she spoke with a cute lisp. "Every time I missed you, I held on to the locket you gave me."

Piper kissed the top of her head. "That's why I gave it to you. The prayer inside is the most important part. A new school calls for lots of prayer, huh?" Maelyn stepped away and nodded, her two braids bouncing on her shoulders. "Are you hungry?"

Maelyn jumped up and down. "Can we go to the hot dog place?"

"Of course. And how about ice cream at the creamery after?"

Maelyn squealed and ran over to pick up her chalk.

"I'll let Grandma know so she can get to work." Piper headed to the open garage, releasing her curls as she took off her hat. The pressure from the hat band remained even after she tossed the hat onto a shelf by the back door. Maybe the pressure wasn't from the hat at all. Piper tried to remind herself that no matter what, life was better than it ever had been. Thanks to Mom and her husband, Bill, and thanks to the Hudsons. Everyone rallied around Piper—and her little girl.

All this came about after a whole bunch of prayer, thanks to her neighbor's Bible study back in Waterloo. If prayer really did work, then Piper had to believe that she was on the right path. A path that would crash into a long, crowded day tomorrow with the occasional appearance of a man she'd never expected to see again.

She grasped her necklace, a match for the one she'd

given Maelyn—a heart-shaped locket with a piece of paper folded up inside that quoted Scripture from Ruth 1:16: *Don't ask me to leave you and turn back. Wherever you will go, I will go... Your God will be my God.* Maelyn's faith had grown fast once Piper had started devotionals with her during Garrett's evening shift, and the little girl's faith was just as big as Piper's—even though Piper's was more of a slow-cooked version, one that was set on low those handful of times she'd ventured to youth group with Sidney in high school. Her faith had only geared up to high and persistent six years later.

Piper said a quick prayer for strength, then looked over her shoulder at her little girl.

At least the next stop on this path had a whole bunch of hugs and giggles, and of course, a few scoops of ice cream.

After taking their ice cream to the town park, they made a quick stop at Jim's grocery—first, to wash off their sticky hands, and second, because Piper needed to buy some groceries for Maelyn's school lunches. By the time they headed home, it was nearly bedtime. Piper glanced in her rearview mirror at Maelyn. Her forehead was pressed to the car window, just like when they'd left the duplex a couple months ago. Maelyn hadn't even looked back. Her little girl had preferred to watch the tall stands of corn in the field across the street instead of the only home she'd ever known. Not much of a home, though. Maelyn's childhood was not the greatest a mom could give to her child. Why would the little girl care to look at the house that had been more like a seven-year time-out for them both?

Piper was glad this night was one more happy step away from all that. "Hey, sweet girl, you must be tired."

"Do I have to go to school tomorrow?" She pressed her nose up on the glass like a little piggy snout.

"Of course. It's a big day for me. First day of work."

The passing streetlights outside brightened Maelyn's face. "Grandma said that she'd bring me to see you there. Said the apple fritters are yummy."

Piper caught herself before saying *absolutely not*. She gave a tight smile and made a mental note to tell Mom to give her time to get used to the work. Piper didn't know how to maneuver this situation quite yet. She was still trying to figure out what was best for her little girl. They had been through so much. Maelyn was still asking questions about Garrett. Not in a way that signaled she missed her stepdad, but in a way that indicated she was making sure they would never have to go back to him.

*Thank you, Lord, that he didn't lay a finger on her... or me.*

As Piper pulled into the dark driveway, she reminded Maelyn, "Let's be quiet, since Papa Bill is sleeping. He gets up super early for work."

Maelyn unbuckled and scooted to the edge of her booster seat. "Quiet as a mouse," she whispered, positioning her hands like claws on either side of her face.

Piper nodded and winked in the rearview mirror but quickly looked away. She'd taught the mouse bit to Maelyn when they'd have to creep through the house while Garrett was sleeping. He hated being woken up. And the yelling that ensued would send little Maelyn to her closet to have a pretend tea party with her dolls while Piper tried calming him down. *Quiet as a mouse* had been code for *quiet, or else*.

Piper opened her door and helped Maelyn out. "Hand me the grocery bag, sweet girl."

Maelyn lugged it from the floorboard with a grunt, handed it over, then hopped down into the cool grass along the driveway.

"You don't have to be super quiet, Mae. Papa won't get mad." Piper squeezed her daughter's shoulder. She'd prayed and prayed that God would fill in the potholes of insecurity that were blasted out by the harsh words spoken from her ex and any angry responses Piper might have dared utter. But mostly, Piper prayed that God would step in and be a daddy to Maelyn, knowing that she really had no idea what that meant. Maelyn had lived with a man who'd only speak to her if she got in the way. To Maelyn, Garrett was more of an indifferent roommate. She had no idea what a father was like. Except she had a pretty good grandfather in Bill.

As they stepped into the yellow glow of the porch light, Maelyn turned around and waited for Piper to unlock the door, putting her finger to her mouth as a sign of silence.

"Just try to be quiet, for kindness' sake." Piper bent down and kissed her head, trying to assure her there was nothing to worry about. They entered the dark living room and headed to the kitchen. Even if Piper didn't quite know how to handle the situation now that Lance would be in her everyday life, she knew one thing for sure. Her main priority was to protect her daughter— to keep her from any other person who might hurt her. She had no guarantee that Lance would happily embrace his unknown child. And Piper was certain he would not have been nearly as kind to her today if he'd known that she'd kept this secret for so long.

# Chapter Three

The next morning, Piper helped Maelyn get ready for school, then drove to work. Yesterday, her chance for a delectable breakfast had been sabotaged by Sidney's text. Not today. She marched straight to the café, her tummy grumbling at the smell of sharp cinnamon melding with butter. Marge, the café manager, was happy to let Piper help herself as she was busy getting everything ready. Piper chose an apple fritter among the display of turnovers, pies and donuts. It was the little things around here—the delicious, homemade, unassuming baked goods—that settled Piper in as if she'd never left.

As she emerged outside again, Sidney appeared at the office door. "Piper! Have you clocked in yet? We are running so behind. The truck had a flat, and we haven't gotten any of the baskets or pickers up to the orchard. We need to load up now."

"No worries. I'll be super fast." Piper jogged past Sid, clocked in and headed out to the truck. Lance was setting stacks of half-peck and quarter-peck baskets into the bed. Piper gathered the telescoping fruit pickers and carried them over to the other side of the truck bed. So many pickers, so many baskets. Lots of people would pour into this place.

"Good morning," she said as the pickers clattered against the metal.

"It's going to be a hot one." Lance squinted up at the sky. "Nothing like breaking a sweat on opening day. Will make it all the more exhausting."

"Sounds great, Mr. Optimism."

Lance paused and stared at her with startled amusement. "Ah, Piper Gray. Ever the jokester."

A loud noise clanked behind them. An employee raised the metal garage door of the corn pool barn across from the café. Piper sucked in a shaky breath. The pool filled with corn kernels was way bigger than any swimming pool she'd seen. Its size was no doubt an indicator of just how many people might traverse these grounds in a day. Any sarcasm she may have offered Lance morphed into nerves.

"Not always a jokester," she said on a breathy, barely committed laugh.

Sidney called out from the café patio, "You all go ahead. Going to help with the initial crowd here."

Lance was already heading to the passenger's side and held open the door for Piper. She held her breath, already fully aware of his cedarwood scent, and her unwelcome stomach flip, and slid into the seat. The truck rumbled and jerked forward. Once they turned up the road to the orchard, the warm breeze poured through the windows.

Piper fiddled with the cool of her silver necklace. "So, there probably won't be too many people today— you know, since it's a school day?" Her nervousness revved with the truck's engine.

Lance shrugged. "Lots of younger families, I guess.

And homeschoolers. There's a big co-op in Rapid Falls. Sidney mentioned hosting an arts and crafts workshop in October." Lance chuckled. "Can't believe how this operation has grown. Who'd have thought we'd stay away to come back to an amusement park?" He shook his head. They passed by the cutouts of nursery-rhyme characters.

"Sidney's always been creative."

Lance nodded in agreement. "She got all of it—the creativity genes, I mean. I am just fine crunching numbers or packaging apples. Nice and straightforward work."

"Not as straightforward as handing a basket and fruit picker to a customer, right?" Piper rubbed her hands on her jeans.

"I sense some uncertainty in your voice?" Lance turned to her with a hooked brow.

Wow, his expression was a grown-up version of Maelyn when she was concerned for her mama. She marveled at the resemblance, until he arched his brows in question.

Piper smiled weakly. "Been a long time since I worked." Or been around so many people. She hoped her dormant extroversion would awaken quickly, because doing her best was important in this fresh start.

"Motherhood is no simple feat, I am sure."

"Oh, that's not work to me."

Lance looked at her again, like he was waiting for her to continue speaking. She only peered out the window.

"Something you and Sidney have in common. Making motherhood seem easy."

"Oh, it's not easy. But I'd never give it up. Maelyn's my world." Piper cleared her throat. This conversation was toeing the edge of her guilty conscience. Lance faced forward. Piper glimpsed his jaw working as they pulled up to the booth.

He put the truck into Park and hopped out. Piper did the same and began to unload the supplies and set them up in the open-air booth.

Her phone trilled in her back pocket. Rapid Falls Elementary popped up on her screen. Piper's stomach dropped, and she walked down by the fence to take the call.

"Hello?"

"Hi, Miss Gray. This is the school nurse. I have Maelyn here with a stomachache. She seems fine, but I told her I would call you."

"Okay. Can I speak with her?" The nurse put Maelyn on the phone.

"Hey, sweet girl, what's going on?"

"Mom, I want to come home." Maelyn's voice wobbled. "The locket's not working."

Piper's throat tightened. "Sweet girl, I… I… I can't get you right now."

"I am having icky thoughts."

Piper shuttered her eyes. This had been a common occurrence since they'd left Waterloo. No doubt, something someone said reminded her of an argument or a mean glare from her stepdad. "That's why I gave you the locket, remember?"

"Uh-huh. It's not working, though."

"Here, let's hold our lockets at the same time. God's with us, sweet girl."

"'K, Mommy."

Piper then explained how she wished she could pick her up right now, but she needed to work. Maelyn seemed to understand and handed the phone to the nurse, and Piper described the anxiety her daughter often faced. The nurse seemed cordial enough and told Maelyn that she could visit her any time during the school day.

"Everything okay?" Lance walked up from the booth.

"Yes, my *world* is just having a cloudy kinda day." She stretched her neck back and forth. "In all seriousness, anxiety is the pits."

"Yes, yes, it is." Lance stuffed his hands in his pocket. "Your little girl has anxiety already?"

Piper hesitated. Did she really want to talk about Maelyn's issues with Lance? She gave a quick tweak of her eyebrows, as if pushing away any further conversation.

Lance seemed to take the hint and waved a hand. "I really know very little about kids. Don't mind me." He straightened some of the baskets. "All right, Piper. You are all set. I'm taking over the hayride for today, so I'd better go get ready. See you at quitting time." Lance headed toward the truck.

Piper gave a flimsy salute. "Hope I don't disappoint you Hudsons."

"All you have to do is smile and hand over the supplies to all those mothers…and their own little worlds." Lance winked, and they both laughed. As he turned to go, his smile fell, and once again, Piper noticed his jaw tighten.

She wondered if he felt as awkward as she did in this unusual reunion. She sighed and began to set up the chalkboard sign on its easel while Lance drove away. Most likely, he had a lot on his mind from the divorce. After all, he had shown up earlier than Don expected, and in the middle of the night without so much as a warning.

Piper wasn't the only one stepping away from her past to embrace being happy this second week of September. She shouldn't feel good about that one thing in common, but at least she felt a little closer to normal. Whatever that was.

Lance hoped to begin to harvest the traditional orchard, but Dad's back was giving him fits, so Lance became the official hayride driver. This was not his vision for the career change from corporate manager to orchard manager. He was a businessman, not a chauffeur to preschoolers. Lance hadn't been surrounded by this many kids in all his adult life. When he was growing up, they'd never had the orchard open to the public. And the youngest person he'd interacted with in Denver was his office's twenty-year-old intern. Today, he had to watch where he stepped for fear of stumbling over three-foot-high bodies.

While he waited to drive the next group, Lance stood closer to the green-and-yellow tractor than the trailer where young parents helped their children up the steps. Better to become an orchard fixture than a liability.

A little boy ran away from his mom and stared up at Lance. "Can I drive up there?"

Lance shook his head. "Sorry, bud. Only me."

His mother was quick to redirect him with a tug on his elbow, and the little guy stomped up the steps with his mom guarding from behind.

Cute kid.

He thought about his conversation with Piper. How she loved her role as a mom but admitted it wasn't easy. Lance had refrained from spilling his guts to Piper— that this past year had begun with the hope to start a family, only for the plan to come crashing down. He didn't want pity, though. He was excited for this next venture—to grow the Hudson legacy in produce sections all across the region. A different kind of family focus.

When the trailer was full, Lance secured the steps. "Everybody, get ready!" he called out, then put on his sunglasses and climbed onto the tractor.

The squeals and giggles from behind were drowned out by the start of the engine. The steady roar and pungent exhaust filled the air while the sun beat down from a cloudless sky. The only shade on the trek to the orchard was near the storage shed. Lance adjusted the little clip-on fan on the side of the tractor's dash so it would blow air on his face. Any day now, the temps would drop to bearable seventies, maybe even mid-sixties, until fall really geared up and everyone would trade their T-shirts for flannels.

The fan blew just right, but something caught his eye. On the white caging of the fan was a black dot. And then something flew toward him. Another black dot landed on his jeans. Suddenly, black splatters coated the clip-on fan and his pants.

As he approached the shady spot a couple hundred feet away from the orchard booth, he slowed to a stop.

"Sorry, folks." Lance twisted in his seat and lifted his cap from his head. "Looks like something needs to be fixed. If you all could just hold on." He turned back in his seat and hopped down, lifting the hood of the tractor. A hose was busted, and oil was splattered all over the machine. Anxiously glancing at the trailer full of people, he pulled out his phone. At least they'd stopped near the shade. The kids were all crowded against that side of the trailer growling and roaring and laughing at the big bad wolf cutout while many of the parents chatted or took pictures.

"Hello?" Dad answered.

"We have a problem. The hose on the tractor busted, and I don't have any tools for a quick fix."

Dad directed Lance to a toolbox stowed at the back of the trailer. "Ah, I found it." Lance opened it and rummaged through tools and materials. "Looks like I have what I need." He turned away from the crowd, lowered his voice and said, "Hope these people don't get too impatient with me. It's been a while since I've gotten my hands this dirty." He laughed, but Dad didn't seem to think it was funny and insisted he would drive out to help. "No, you stay. We can't afford for your back to get worse. Don't worry. I've got—"

"Hey, Lance." Piper walked up with a basketful of apples.

Lance pushed his phone against his chest. "Hey, Piper. Who's helping at the booth?"

"I just put up the little sign Sidney made…says Be Back in a Peck." Piper grinned. "She told me to use it whenever I needed to step away. No biggie. I saw you here with the hood up on the tractor… Figured I might help? Want me to guide the folks up to the orchard? Maybe coax them with a free apple?" She nodded to the basket in her arms.

"That's great thinking." Lance filled Dad in and ended the call. "I take it your jitters have worn off?"

"It's been a great day so far. And I know how to keep kids happy. Has a lot to do with snack time." Familiar humor brightened her countenance and brought about an unexpected calm. She headed over to the trailer, and Lance unlatched the steps, all the while convincing himself his reaction to Piper was induced only by her quick thinking and nothing more.

"Hey, folks, our orchard attendant will guide you the rest of the way. Sorry about the inconvenience." The chattering crowd grew louder, and everyone exited the trailer in an orderly fashion. Piper handed an apple to each parent.

Lance assured everyone as they passed, "By the time you all get your apples picked, we'll have the trailer up and running."

Piper smiled big. She leaned toward him as she surveyed the crowd and muttered, "Any chance you have a nice singing voice? I am thinking the best way to get these littles to move in a timely way is to Pied Piper it." Her green eyes narrowed into thin slits as she giggled.

"Suits you best, I think... *Piper*." He chuckled and strode back to the tractor.

As he got to work, he glanced up and watched Piper lead the group. She was talking to a couple of little girls with braids as if they were straight out of *Little House on the Prairie*, although they wore jean shorts and T-shirts—no aprons or lace-up boots. For someone who seemed nervous to get back in the workforce, Piper appeared at ease and eager to help make this hiccup seem like part of the experience.

Lance was able to fix the problem before the return crowd got too large. Only a few customers waited on the benches along the road. He pulled up and parked under some more shady trees, hopped out and positioned the steps. "I'll be right back, folks, if you want to go ahead and get settled." He jogged over to the booth.

Piper was helping a customer unload a small wagon of apples into some baskets.

"I'm going to make some apple butter for the Rapid Falls Harvest Festival. Do you have any flyers or business cards I can set out?" the young woman asked.

"Uh, just a sec." Piper scurried back into the booth

and rummaged through some of the stuff on the shelves beneath the counter. "I think you can definitely ask at the main building…"

Lance leaned on the counter. "Yep, that's the best thing to do. Sidney probably has plenty of flyers."

Piper popped up from her crouched position. "Oh, I didn't see you, Lance. Is everything okay?"

"Yeah, got the tractor fixed for now. How is it going?"

Piper gave a thumbs-up, then hurried out of the booth and helped the customer load up her wagon with the filled baskets. "Be careful not to tip that thing. You sure you want to walk back?"

The customer nodded. "No big deal." She smiled and started down the dirt road. "I do it every year," she called over her shoulder.

"Every year?" Lance muttered then whistled. "All three of the years we've been open to the public, I guess." He smirked, leaning into the shade of the booth, clasping his fingers on the edge of the counter. "This is quite the operation out here, huh?"

They both surveyed the rows of trees dotted about with people, mostly with their noses pointed to the fruit-laden branches.

"It's peaceful." Piper sighed.

"I'm glad it's been a good first day."

"Thanks." Her smile was breathtaking. Thankfully, Lance had just exhaled. No breath to be taken. "My biggest issue was a telescoping fruit picker that wouldn't telescope." She shrugged her shoulders, then the corner of her mouth twitched. "And having to bail you out of a wagon full of preschoolers and flustered parents."

Instead of analyzing why his pulse jumped slightly at this woman's way with teasing, he offered a practical defense. "My duties are acquiring distributors, packaging produce and loading it for transport. This is not my cup of…cider?" He rolled his eyes at the silly joke, stuck his hands in his back pockets and stepped away. "Glad you knew what to do. I would have just had the customers wait on me."

Piper stared, as if she were the one waiting on him… to retract the statement? Had he said something wrong? He opened his mouth, but Piper blurted, "The patience of a three-year-old is about as small as an apple seed. You've got to be quick in this line of work." She tapped her head and winked.

"I guess I need to learn from you, Pied Piper?" He steadied his gaze on the beautiful young mother, allowing his smile to grow. Piper's amused look faded into one of—anticipation? Lance's chest constricted. His playfulness was trying to rival Sid's newest additions. How unlike his usual businessman countenance. Piper opened her mouth to speak, but Lance resumed a more practical tone. "Just kidding. It won't be necessary once Dad's better." He began to walk back to the trailer. "Just making sure all was well here. I'll get back to it."

If there was one thing that stood out in Lance's mind from the days leading up to his stumbling romance with Piper, it was her wit and quick thinking, always offering amusing banter that deflected the seriousness of any mishap.

While he once thought it was cute, he didn't have the patience of an apple seed, or a whole apple tree, to keep up with Piper Gray out here in the heat. His old reactions to this woman had taken him off guard more than once this afternoon. He was definitely not taking tips from the one person who'd made leaving Rapid Falls difficult in the first place.

# Chapter Four

The last group of customers piled onto the hayride with arms full of apples, sippy cups and diaper bags. Piper checked the time. 4:02. Maelyn should be getting off the bus any minute. Piper stepped through the gate to the orchard to be sure no supplies were left out. The trees marched ahead, still heavy with fruit but surrounded by plenty of fallen apples. She spied a step stool at the far end and jogged over. In the small valley on the far side of the orchard, Piper noticed the work truck. Sidney tromped through pumpkin vines, placing little signs along the way. Piper couldn't help but smile. Then a rush of emotion surprised her.

How long had it been since Piper had taken time to breathe fresh air, enjoy the quiet of nature and focus on someone else's joy? Sure, she'd often revel in Maelyn's sweet milestones and cute childish ways, but with every smile Piper had managed, there had been a string of guilt tugging down her lips, harnessing any happiness with the threat of disappointment. Piper shaded her eyes and looked west toward Rapid Falls. Now she could truly enjoy Maelyn knowing that Garrett had no

influence on her. Piper was proud of herself for dismantling the harness at last.

Sidney was waving her arms in her direction. Piper
snapped out of her thoughts and waved back. Sidney
then pulled her phone out, and Piper's phone rang.

"Hey, Sidney."

"Piper! Don't you dare walk back by yourself. I want
to know how everything went today. I'll be up in just
a minute."

"Okay, sounds good." Piper grinned as she ended the
call. She could feel her own spirit ripening more and
more, like the fruit on the trees—sweet and purpose-
ful, and full of joy with no strings attached.

After putting away the step stool, Piper walked toward the truck as it appeared around the bend.

Sidney pulled over, and Piper hopped in. "I was
going to try and come chat with you at lunch today,"
Sidney said as she shifted from Park to Drive. "But
there was all sorts of confusion in the café that needed
clearing up. Supposedly, folks don't want to spend ten
dollars on a jug of apple cider but are willing to spend
four dollars on a gift basket of jams and cookies." She
rolled her eyes. "The price tag mix-up put a huge snag
in things."

"That's tough," Piper agreed. "No worries about
lunch. I enjoyed keeping to myself. Haven't been around
so many people in a long time. A lunch for one was a
nice break."

Sidney slid a leery gaze in her direction. "You've
changed, Piper. I can't help but remember the last play-
off game for the Rapid Falls Eagles. You were smack-
dab in the middle of the bleachers hooting and hollering
at those Polk Center Raiders."

Piper sighed. "It was a rough go before, but I am

feeling like myself more and more." She thought about that harness of disappointment in the life she'd chosen with Garrett—and, by default, had given to her little girl. Garrett had criticized Piper plenty over their eight years, knocking that fun-loving, extroverted teen right out of her skin. "As always, Hudson Orchard is steady ground."

Sidney nodded. "You sound like Todd. He always quotes that verse in the Bible about building your house on sand versus rock. He says we're built on a rock." She took a deep breath and continued, "But Piper, I am worried about you. I know you said you'll share more later. Please tell me—you and Maelyn aren't in any danger, are you?"

"Oh, no." She locked a sincere gaze with Sidney's questioning one. "Garrett has totally moved on. Promise."

"Really? Even from Maelyn?"

Piper's steadiness faltered. Garrett knew Mae wasn't his from the start. "He just wasn't attached to us like he should've been. Don't worry. It's all settled." She rolled down the window and dangled her fingers in the warm breeze. "But what I am wondering most is why your brother is such a humbug about this place?" Sidney's groan ensured that Piper had successfully diverted the conversation away from herself.

"What did Lance say? He's been grumbly about the entertainment factor around here."

"That it's—" Piper made air quotes with her fingers and said, "Not his cup of cider," then drummed them together and put on a silly impression—like a detective on a black-and-white TV show. "You see, my dear Hudson, he seems to want to sit in a dark warehouse and package apples instead."

"Sounds about right," Sidney confirmed. "Just wait 'til the pumpkin patch is ready. That will lighten him up."

They parked in front of the metal building. After clocking out, Piper waited for Lance to pull out of the private driveway first, then she headed to her car. She was done conversing. With everyone. All her energy had been zapped by that little punching sound on her time card.

She was officially off the clock and anxious to get back to Maelyn.

The sun played peekaboo with the tree lines and hills as she headed toward Rapid Falls. At least there were still a few hours left of daylight. Maelyn would want to play outside after dinner.

Piper pulled into the driveway and noticed two bare feet poking out on the other side of the hedge by the front door. When Piper walked up, Maelyn was sitting with her elbows on her knees and her face in her hands. Her shoes and socks were tossed on the porch.

"Maelyn?"

Her daughter's head jerked up. "Mommy!" She sprang to her feet and wrapped her arms around Piper's waist. Muffled sniffles and whimpers jolted Piper's heart.

"What's the matter, sweet girl?"

Maelyn pulled away, her eyes filled with tears. "Nobody's home."

"What?" Blood drained from Piper's face. She noticed Maelyn's backpack on the rocking chair by the front door. "You've been here for an hour? Alone?" Maelyn nodded, little dimples dotting her chin beneath a quivering lip.

"Oh, I am so sorry, Maelyn." Piper's pulse raced at the thought of her seven-year-old being alone all this time. She was certain she'd clarified the schedule with Mom. She pulled Maelyn close again and fished her phone out of her back pocket, then scrolled through the text exchange with Mom.

You sure you can be here for Maelyn after school? I don't get off 'til 5.

Yep. Planning on it.

Okay, thanks, Mom.

Sure thing.

What had gone wrong? Suddenly, Piper's concern shifted from Maelyn's well-being to Mom's circumstances. She said a little prayer of protection over Mom just as a car pulled into the driveway. Mom waved from behind the steering wheel and disappeared into the garage.

"Come on, Mae. Let's get you a snack."

Her daughter grabbed the backpack while Piper unlocked the front door. Besides frustration squeezing Piper's throat, a nagging sense of déjà vu had her walk slightly unsteady.

"He-llooo?" Mom's singsong greeting from the other side of the kitchen wall was much too pleasant. She appeared around the corner. Her work visor was nestled amid her graying red curls. "How are my favorite girls?"

"Not great, Mom," Piper muttered and pushed Maelyn along to the kitchen table. She pulled out a box of crackers from the cabinet and a string cheese from the fridge. "Here, sweet girl. I am going to talk with Grandma for a sec. Get yourself some water, too."

Maelyn exhaled a choppy breath, reiterating the emotional toll of being locked out and obviously forgotten.

Piper tugged at Mom's elbow as they stepped into the living room.

"What's going on?" Mom whispered.

Piper spun around, planting her fists on her hips. "You tell me. I thought you'd be here when Maelyn got off the bus."

"She gets off at 5, right?"

"No. That's me."

"What, that's not what I..." She looked at her phone screen and shook her head. "Oh, darling. I... I must have read the text wrong." Mom looked over her shoulder at Maelyn, who was peeling string cheese and swinging her legs beneath her chair. Piper released the rest of her pent-up air. At least Maelyn seemed settled now. "I was just so busy today and didn't read the text carefully." She raked her hand through the wild curls sprouting from her visor. The worry lines that no doubt had grown deep and long during the days with that bullish man she'd once been married to appeared from the corners of her eyes. Her lip wobbled, just as it had done most days back when her ex would throw his voice from one end of the house to the other. "It won't happen again, Piper." She then bolted across the floor and wrapped her arms around Maelyn.

"Oh, my sweet thing. You know Grandma loves you so much!" She planted a giant kiss on Maelyn's forehead. "Think we should make bagel pizzas tonight?"

Piper shook her head and joined Maelyn at the table, nearly tripping over the corner of the rug sprawled out on the linoleum. Huh. She wondered how much had been swept under that rug besides crumbs from bagel pizzas? A whole lot of apologies and conversations were no doubt shoved beneath their feet.

An apology from Mom had been hard to come by

when she was younger, and now Mom skipped on to dinner plans with Mae. Piper had longed for her mother to acknowledge the hurt her previous husband had inflicted on Piper during high school. But Mom had just moved onto the next thing, seemingly ignoring Piper all the more. Exactly why Piper felt like she had no choice but to move away, and later, why she hadn't felt comfortable sharing her own marital woes with her mom.

Mom just didn't seem to think it necessary to work through hard things—or talk about them.

Unexpectedly, Piper had a craving for all things apple, and the old longing to escape to Hudson Orchard rose from her toes to her nose, just like it had when she was younger. Some days, she would go straight from school to Sidney's home. The desire to immerse herself in Hudson comfort was ever strong. Only, now, she was fighting off the urge. Piper's life was here, sitting right across from her, anchoring her to this place, no matter if she'd once escaped as often as she could.

"How was work, Piper?" Mom asked as she placed bagels on a toaster oven tray.

"Actually, pretty good."

"For now, I guess," Mom added. "Seasonal work is not ideal."

"Wow. I never knew you to say how you felt outright, Mom." Piper made a silly face at Maelyn to be sure to mask her annoyance.

Mom just shrugged. "Well, it's not."

"I know." They'd had this discussion briefly when Piper had told Mom about Sidney's offer. Mom didn't understand what life was like for Piper back in Waterloo. Nor why she might need to ease into work life again. Unfortunately, while Piper and Maelyn were at Garrett's financial mercy, Mom had been struggling to get out from under bankruptcy. Most of the time Piper had called to get advice, she would end up giving Mom advice. Bill had helped. Piper was overjoyed that her stepdad Bill was part of Mom's life now. She deserved to be happy after the nightmare of a marriage before. If only Mom had met Bill after Piper's dad had passed away when she was an infant.

"So, I think cubed ham and pineapple would be delish on this. Don't you, Mae?" Mom changed the topic once again.

"Ew. I don't think so," Maelyn lisped with a scrunched nose and eyes begging for Piper's rescue.

Piper laughed and blew away all the building resentment. Or, more likely, swept it swiftly under the carpet at their feet.

After a couple of days filling in for Dad, Lance finally got to start a workday in the production role he'd signed on to. After a morning in the orchard, he returned to the main area and unloaded wood bins of apples with the forklift by the metal building.

A familiar voice called out from the direction of the nearby café patio, "Lance Hudson. You're here!"

Lance glanced over his shoulder. Tony Emerson's full-on smile beneath his Iowa Hawkeyes baseball cap flung Lance back a decade. "Tony. Good to see you!" He turned the machinery off and walked up to his best friend from middle and high school. They shook hands. "Got the day off?"

Tony turned around and held out his hand to a tall blond woman wearing a maternity sundress, her hand splayed on her rounded torso. "My wife's due date is today. So, we thought walking around the orchard would help us get closer to meeting the newest Emerson." Tony introduced his wife, Callie, then asked, "Are you back for good?"

"Looks like it. Dad needed a business manager for the production side of things." Lance stuck his hands in his pockets and glanced beyond the public area to the acreage reserved for distribution to local stores. "I want to keep the production side thriving."

"Well, that's a coincidence."

"What do you mean?"

"I've been assistant manager to Jim at the grocery store but just got an opportunity to move up to produce manager with Clyde's supermarket chain." *Clyde's?* That was one of the chains Lance had researched. "They've expanded into midsize towns across the eastern part of Iowa. Thankfully, their offices are in Waterloo, so not too far of a commute."

"Wow, and Jim's okay with losing you?"

"He's fully supportive. Has some great staff to choose from to fill my spot."

"He's always been such a gem in Rapid Falls," Callie added.

"That's the truth," Lance agreed. He may have left for a good long while, but he sure felt like he could pick up right where he'd left off with Rapid Falls folks.

Tony filled him in on some of the guys they used to hang out with, while Lance led the way toward the hayride where Dad was getting situated for his first round. Tony helped his wife up to sit on a hay bale closest to the steps.

Tony asked, "Are you all looking for new stores to stock?"

"That's my goal." Since the you-pick business model brought in plenty of revenue, and Dad wanted to semi-retire, he had been willing to minimize their grocery distribution. But Grandpa Jo had started the orchard for wider distribution all along. Lance was willing and able to make that family dream come true. "We'd like to continue to supply produce wherever we can."

"That's what I figured. So, how about we talk with my contact at Clyde's and see what he would think about Hudson Orchard? They're really pushing for local produce, and you all have such a great operation here."

"You'd do that?" Just this morning, Lance had felt behind because he hadn't made one business call. He'd even thought about sending up some prayer. But that just wasn't his go-to anymore. It hadn't helped one bit when he needed it most.

"Jim is not the only gem in this area. Your parents have been so helpful on city council and keeping traditions alive in town. Like the Harvest Festival. You know, some folks tried to get rid of it, but your parents sought outside sponsorship and now the festival is visited by folks from all over northeast and central Iowa."

"I am sure Sidney had a lot to do with that." His family was definitely a crop of go-getters. And he was so thankful for their persistence. Lance wouldn't have ever had the nerve to go to college across the country if his parents hadn't supported him one hundred and ten percent. Returning to Rapid Falls wasn't only a homecoming with his family but a revisiting of a place of old friendships with loyalty as abundant as their apples.

Tony gave Lance his new business card, and they arranged for a conference call with Tony and his new boss later.

"All dependent on the baby's decision to arrive." Tony winked.

"Of course." Lance nodded. Callie was fanning herself with a wide-brimmed straw hat. "You'd better get her back to some decent shade. Thanks, Tony." Lance returned to the forklift, excited to get these apples unloaded and possibly begin a brand-new order.

Out of the corner of his eye, he saw Piper and Sidney exit the café, chatting away as they carried to-go cups to the work truck. Piper looked over at him and gave her silly salute once again, just like yesterday.

That woman was ever a jokester. Full of life. She was certainly doing just fine around here. And she was exactly where she needed to be—on the amusement side of Hudson Orchard with all those little kids running about. Curiosity swelled as he marveled at the woman. What was she like around her daughter? He suspected she glowed.

Lance shook off his old habit of getting lost in his thoughts and focused on the forklift controls. The new opportunity with Clyde's was assurance that he'd grown past daydreaming. His business plan was becoming a reality. As easy as pie—apple pie, of course.

# Chapter Five

The next morning, Lance grabbed a piece of toast and headed to the metal building, excited to start on their newest order after a successful conference call yesterday.

Dad was pouring diesel into the tractor. "Good morning, son. Where've you been all these years?" he teased. "Still in shock that you got in with Clyde's." He whistled. "Imagine. Tony and you working together again—after all those youth group service projects."

"And to think, I almost missed seeing him at all. Was just dropping off the last of row N. Would have been in the orchard most of the day after that. I'd have never known about his in with Clyde's," Lance said and sipped from his travel mug. "Amazing coincidence."

"There are no coincidences, son. Just confirmation that you were in the right place at the right time." Dad winked. "Guess you didn't miss out on much when my back gave me fits after all."

"I am glad your back is better now. I can get to work. I have a crew lined up to help." Lance felt more like himself today. He had a specific task that would keep him busy doing what he loved. While he prepped the warehouse for packaging, Sidney walked Piper through the production process, explaining how everything worked.

"I really don't see you needing to do any of this, Piper," Sidney repeated. "But it's good to know if customers have questions."

"Sounds good." Piper folded her arms across her chest. "So…shouldn't I get up to the orchard booth?"

Sidney smiled wide, just like when she used to ask Lance for a favor—like running her to the store when her car was out of gas or letting her have the first pick of Mom's cookies.

"Actually, I was kinda hoping you would help me with the school field trip that's going to arrive—" the sound of loud bus brakes squealed outside "—this very minute." Sidney rushed to the door. "I just need someone to walk them up to the orchard. I had one of our other employees get the booth set up earlier. Do you think you could share info about the orchard, Piper?" Sidney handed Piper a laminated sheet. "This is pretty much a script. Say it word for word or add your own flair. You know about this place."

"I'm no public speaker, Sid." Piper bounced a nervous look between Lance and Sidney.

"Piper, you were great with the families when the tractor broke down," Lance added.

"You'll be awesome," Sidney affirmed. "And you get to start off in here, with Lance. He'll be the main speaker. Right, Lance?"

"What? I'm starting a new order today."

"Perfect. Then you can share the process."

Lance shook his head. "Sid, I'm just about to head out and instruct the crew. They can come by later, but really, I can't be a tour guide today."

"Oh, come on, brother. It's our family business,

after all." Sidney snagged a rolled-up piece of paper and pressed it out on the powered-down conveyer belt. She thumped a finger on the pumpkin patch plans. "Instead of turning the carriage into a pumpkin, I turned a whole acre into pumpkins." She nudged him. "Think about all the work I put into making your pumpkin patch dream come true."

He towered over the plans and splayed his hands on either side, trying to avoid the scowl that was initiated by Sid's words *dream come true*. It was as if his twin had taken an old line that he'd weeded from his conscience and now hit him in the heart with it.

"Listen, sis. This isn't a dream come true until I see a gazebo smack-dab in the middle." He crammed his finger on the plan. "That's my dream come true." He smirked, then lifted his chin up in a smug, not-going-to-budge way. His eyes landed on the one person he'd forgotten was connected to his reason for wanting a gazebo. Piper caught his stare and crinkled her brow in question. Had she forgotten the afternoon before the fireworks show when they'd painted the gazebo at the city park? It had been for a service project. Sure, Lance had suggested the service project at youth group because his granddad had built the gazebo back in the fifties. But the structure took on a whole new significance when his first kiss was with Piper Gray that very afternoon, beneath freshly painted trim.

Lance's pulse raced wildly at the memory. It had everything to do with the woman standing before him with sparkly eyes and a stray curl that was tempting him to sweep it away.

Sidney tilted her head. "C'mon, Lance. That's where the turnabout is for the hayride."

"You should have filled me in before any of this came to fruition."

"Oh, just like you showing up a couple months early?"

"That was spontaneity at its finest." Lance caught Piper's nod in agreement with Sidney. "Piper, you don't think that was a good surprise?" For his family, at least.

"What, you returning to Rapid Falls?" Piper scoffed. "Oh, let us all jump for joy that the guy who thought he was older and wiser than all of us moved back to tell us what to do." Piper waved her hands in the air and widened her eyes in faint surprise at what she'd just said.

Sidney burst out laughing. Lance stepped back and chuckled. "Someone had to make sure you all made it to the next birthday."

"We did. And we have lots of fun stories, too." Piper slid her arm through Sidney's bent elbow. "But please, don't tell my daughter about the time we climbed on the elementary school roof. She loves to climb trees. That would be a thrilling feat for her, I am sure."

Sidney beamed, admiring her best friend. Lance wondered if Piper had forgotten about their whirlwind romance. She had brought up a lot of memories from before that. Would she dare bring up their summer love? Lance felt heat creep up his neck as he thought about how awkward that might be.

"So… Lance, pretty please show the kids how apple production works?" Sidney's brow went up in several pleading folds.

Lance dropped his shoulders. "Okay. But—" He held up a finger. "Only because it's educational and a good experience for kids to see hard work. I still remember when we went on a field trip to the John Deere headquarters. Sparked my interest in production." He pulled out his phone to text the crew. "Maybe a kid will be inspired."

"That's the way to think about it." Sidney began to roll up the plans. "You aren't just a business manager. You're a dream maker, Lance."

"Dreaming is one thing. Giving a kid a vision for a successful future—that's another. What grade?"

"Second grade. They've come every fall since we opened to the public. You'll do great, Lance."

Piper bit her lip as if she had something to say and refrained from doing so.

Lance hooked an eyebrow in her direction. "Well?"

She exhaled a breath that lifted that ridiculously cute curl, then tapped her chin. "What's that saying?" She shifted her gaze upward as if trying to gather her thoughts. "If you don't have anything nice to say…" Her snark was fully present and enticing.

Sidney giggled and Lance rolled his eyes. "I was afraid you would say that I would put those kids to sleep." Lance chuckled, thinking that was just what the old Piper might have said to him.

Piper laughed a little too forcefully to be sincere. "I'll be right back to help with the kids, Sid." She hurried to the office, phone in hand.

"Looks like I struck a nerve," Lance muttered, watching Piper focused on her cell.

"Her daughter's in second grade." Sidney's eyes lit up. "Maybe she's here today!" His sister rushed over to the office and said something to Piper, and Piper shook her head. Her lips were pale, and once again, Lance could see slight nervousness in her expression.

Unease flipped his stomach as he put away the drawing and began to set up for the next round of packaging. He sure hoped Piper was up for this today. He didn't want to be pulled away from production once again, trekking alongside a group of kids like she had done for him. But even though he focused on the inconvenience her absence might cause, he didn't like seeing Piper's fiery personality extinguish so quickly.

She exited the office with a look of relief.

"Everything okay, Piper?"

"Oh, yes. I thought I'd forgotten Maelyn's field trip day. But it's next week. Unfortunately, she has an appointment, so she'll miss it." She disappeared outside. Before Lance could add sanitizer to the tank, Piper was back, leading a group of kids and teachers into the room.

Once the teachers helped each student settle, Lance gave his demonstration on how they washed the apples and prepped them for packaging. The group conversed quietly, jotting notes on their clipboards. Piper was crouched down next to a little boy who seemed to have a hard time holding his pencil. She was pointing to his worksheet and spelling words for him. Her rust red hair clashed with his bright red T-shirt. He seemed completely at ease after she stood up and patted his shoulder.

"Once again, Piper-the-Great to the rescue," Lance remarked as she helped guide the rest of the group toward the doors.

She kept her attention on the kids. "How so?"

"Helping that little boy."

"It's not hard to do," she said, glancing his way. "Helping kids is not nearly as difficult as trying to help adults."

"I can see that." He recalled their senior year together, when Piper would confide in him about her anger toward her stepfather, and he would share his fears about moving away from his family. Sidney was away at camp, so most afternoons Piper and Lance spent time together. "But you did try to help your mom, no matter how difficult. Seems it finally worked."

Piper gaped at him. "You remember that?"

"Of course. We had written the note together. You used to say how special letter-writing was. You still have your dad's letters to you as a baby?"

Piper nodded, her eyes rounding. "Lance," she whispered, then cleared her throat and spoke in a soft voice. "You are the only one besides Mom that knows about those. I almost forgot."

Lance rubbed her arm. "Hey, I rarely forget important things. Sometimes it's not a good trait." He chuckled and shoved his hands in his pockets. "They stay important in my mind when others have moved on." Like all the loving moments he thought his ex-wife Tara would treasure, too.

A look of consideration narrowed Piper's eyes. One that twinged his chest with a reminiscent pain. Piper had moved on when he hadn't been ready to.

"Lance, thanks for not forgetting." She scrunched her button nose. "It's nice to be known, huh?"

A teacher told Piper they were ready to continue. She ran back to the counter by the front door, grabbed her laminated script and waved it at Lance as she passed. "Guess I could use some help. Always forgetful." She waggled her eyebrows and raced ahead of the students.

She continued outside but spun around and added, "You know, Lance, I think a gazebo is a really great idea."

"You…do?" Had his voice just cracked? Wow, this was an unexpected compliment from the woman who knew him way back when his voice had yet to crack.

"Yeah. I think it would be a nice addition to your amazingly spectacular pumpkin patch." Her tone was humorous, and her smile sparkled like she'd just answered a question at a beauty contest. Yes, she was beautiful, indeed.

"So, I am a little rusty on decoding Piper-speak." Lance walked over to her and tilted his head to be sure he heard correctly. He'd forgotten how short she was or, maybe, how tall he had become. Until he'd returned to his childhood home, Lance had felt about the size of a gnat most days. "Are you serious that you think it's a good idea?"

Piper tossed her red curly-top head back and chuckled. "Sheesh, Mr. Serious-o, take a compliment. Yes. Good idea. My little girl is fascinated by gazebos. I think lots of kids would be." She gave a nonchalant lift of her shoulders, then left with the group of school kids.

Lance rubbed the back of his neck and forced himself to look away from the newest Hudson Orchard employee. He also forced himself to not pull out the plan for the pumpkin patch and try and squeeze in a gazebo for a little girl he'd never met.

But if he was honest with himself, was it really for Piper's little girl?

He peered over his shoulder and spotted Piper walking backward with the laminated sheet in one hand and pointing to the corn pool with her other. The class followed along. How could Lance even consider doing anything for Piper, or anyone outside of his safe circle of family?

The good thing about returning to this place was that all those who loved him shed light on the misconception of how small he'd felt back in Denver. But there was something Denver had taught him that had stuck.

There was no use wasting energy on trying to figure someone out or learning how to keep up with another's quirks. Because no matter how much Lance had dedicated to being ever-willing to understand his ex-wife—to do what was best for her and a future family—he was left blindsided in the end, feeling gullible and betrayed.

Not worth it.

He looked around the familiar warehouse. Empty crates, ready to be packed with produce, leaned up against the back wall, slightly crooked and banged up after years of use. From a square window, the assigned acreage for traditional production bathed in the morning sunlight, waiting for Lance and a small crew to harvest for their newest client.

Lance clapped his hands together. "Time to work." Excitement filled his chest. This was what he'd left Colorado for. To elevate his family business. To pour every ounce of his thinking into doing a job well done.

Piper was amazed with herself. Being able to lead this tour, words pouring from her lips, all the while her insides rattling with her pounding pulse. Lance Hudson embodied the season in their relationship that, for Piper, bloomed with affection and trust in her best friend's brother. She'd swept their connection away when things got complicated—like a positive pregnancy test and her ex-boyfriend Garrett wanting to make amends. She became more like Piper-the-Mess, not Piper-the-Great. Did Lance remember the reason they'd written the letter to her mom back then? It had been because Piper was going to be kicked out of the house after graduation, thanks to her stepdad's request. Lance had encouraged Piper to share her frustrations with her mom—

Piper finished reading the first paragraph on the laminated sheet and paused. She stared at the white space, then ogled in the direction of the metal building. She and Lance had read her old letters and created the new one after they'd painted the gazebo in the city park. Her cheeks heated as she spied Lance moving about the work space.

The day of their first kiss.

Did their first kiss at the gazebo have anything to do with his dream of having one now?

"Nah," she muttered.

All the students and teachers stared at her.

"Sorry, folks! Let's move on." The next paragraph in her script confirmed her assumption was absolutely false. "The patriarch of the Hudson Family, Joseph, contributed much to Rapid Falls, including building the gazebo at the center of the city park." Family tradition, these gazebos. That was all. It was purely coincidental that their first kiss was at a gazebo and that Lance insisted they include a gazebo in the pumpkin patch. Piper needed to continue to focus on the here and now.

The teachers interrupted the tour with some redirecting of the squirrely kids in the back of the group just as they headed down the dirt lane to the orchard. Piper was so focused on the laminated sheet in her hands, she didn't notice a dip in the ground.

Her foot slipped, her ankle twisted and she fell on her backside. "Ow!"

Gasps and little voices asked if she was okay. The two teachers rushed over and helped her up.

"I—I think I am fine, really."

"Are you sure?" the younger teacher with a blond ponytail asked in a high-pitched voice that made Piper feel like an eight-year-old, not a grown woman.

"Really." But when she stepped forward to pick up her laminated sheet, a shot of pain made her double over and clutch at the baggy sleeves of the teacher's sweatshirt. "Ouch!" From the corner of her eye, she saw Lance's strides gobbling up the grassy knoll where the class huddled around her. Piper did not need to be rescued. She stood up as best as she could, squinting and biting the inside of her cheek. But the pain in her throbbing ankle was so much worse than her molars' vicelike grip.

Lance spoke quietly with the teachers, then slipped his arm around Piper's shoulders. She flinched involuntarily. Of course, she didn't have anything against the strong arm of Lance Hudson conforming to her frame. Piper stole a sideways look to see if he'd noticed her flinch. He seemed most concerned with the squabbling kids.

Good.

Long ago, Piper's flurry of anticipation for such a comforting gesture by him had been a usual feeling. But since then, she'd been trained to not need comfort. How many times had Garrett hurt her with words or taking away her means to buy groceries? Longing for comfort only seemed weak and unattainable.

Lance cleared his throat and announced, "We've had a change of plans, kids. Instead of the orchard first, how about a dip in the corn pool?" The kids cheered.

"Wow, pure Iowan love of corn, huh?" Piper jested, then winced as she tried to shift her weight.

Lance's grip grew firm, and this time, she didn't flinch. Maybe, just maybe, she could lean into him. Only because she was breaking a sweat from the pain. Well, not really a sweat, but a slight misting. Of course, she wasn't a hundred percent sure it was all because of her ankle and not because of this man next to her, someone she'd shut out of her life—for his own good, in fact. He had had big plans, and she'd known that a girl like Piper Gray was not someone who deserved to be part of those plans. Especially not if her news would mess up those west coast college plans. Even so, no matter their muddled past, she knew that Lance Hudson was a good guy. And right now, he was there without any ultimatums or stifling control issues.

Lance was holding on to her because she needed help.

She leaned into him as he gently guided her down the hill, while the teachers led the kids to the corn pool. Just this once, Piper would allow herself to be in someone's care.

"Let's head to the house. It's not any farther than the office if we cross here, and Mom will know what to do."

"That's right. Nurse Janet. Hope retirement didn't squelch her skills."

"Never."

"That's what I figured. She's amazing." Piper managed a calm tone, although her heart was racing. Must be the pesky pain getting to her. Nothing to do with Lance's cologne of cedar and mint, or his gentle *excuse me*s to customers as they crossed their path.

As soon as they got to the privacy fence that separated the public entrance from the Hudson's side yard, Piper held onto the fence post and insisted she could make it on her own.

"Are you sure?" Lance held open the gate, and she hopped through.

"It's all good. I've always been a good hopper. See?" She hopped in a circle. "Remember when we had to jump rope in gym class? My expertise was one-footed jumping."

He stepped closer and grasped her arms. "Piper, let me help you."

"I don't need help," she muttered. Her throat closed as he seemed to study her mouth. "No! I am just fine." She pushed away, and Lance stepped back, gesturing for her to go ahead.

Piper managed the rest of the way but then crashed all her weight against the side door. "I'm fine!" she called out, her nose skimming the door. "Meant to do that."

Lance hooked his hand under her elbow, chuckling. "Sure you did. Ever the clown."

Piper looked up at him in scorn but miscalculated her defense. He was so close, and his blue eyes were tender and attentive. Her sassy smirk dissolved into a lazy grin. Lance raised an eyebrow as if he were waiting for her to respond, but his parting lips made her question what either of them should be thinking in this moment. Where was the gazebo now? A reunion kiss? That would be absolutely—

"Piper," Lance spoke softly.

"Yes?" Her heart was now in her throat and her ankle felt as though it were hovering above the ground below—far, far away.

"You are leaning against the doorknob. Are we going to go inside, or what?" He narrowed his gaze across the front yard to the distant…horizon? Parking lot? Anywhere but here with the silly Piper Gray?

"Right," Piper mumbled and steadied herself as she grasped the doorknob, shook Lance's hand off her elbow, pushed open the door and hopped inside.

Janet was sitting at the kitchen island with a roll of

postage stamps and a stack of postcards. "Well, hello, you two. This is an unexpected visit."

Lance pulled out a stool and pressed a hand on Piper's back.

"I am fine by myself, Lance." Piper jerked the stool farther out from the counter and plopped down on it, turning her full attention to the sweet woman across from her. "Clumsy me. I twisted my ankle."

"Oh, no!" Janet pushed her red-rimmed glasses up through her salt-and-pepper hair. The gray only enhanced Janet Hudson's grace, and the smile lines fanning out from her blue eyes only marked her distinguished—a definition of Mrs. Hudson, the mother of two amazing twins and the second mother to Piper for many days of her school years. Janet scraped her stool along the tiled floor. "Here, hon. Prop it up on my knee."

Lance must have learned his gentleness from his mother. She had a way of zoning in on the most urgent need and sending out waves of tranquility and assurance that all would be well. Had she learned that in nursing school?

Lance sat at the round kitchen table in the breakfast nook and planted his elbow on his knee and his chin in his palm. Same concern and focus. Maybe it wasn't nursing school but a dazzling trait passed down from the previous Hudson generation. Those Hudsons. Piper sighed, then tried to ignore the flush creeping up across her chest as both sets of Hudson eyes gazed at her. She stared at her ankle.

After a brief examination, which included Piper minimally squawking when Janet touched the sore spot, Janet suggested, "It seems like you just tweaked it. The best thing is to stay off it as much as possible. Lance, will you go get those crutches from the utility room?"

"Crutches?" Piper blurted out while Lance crossed over to the hallway on the other side of the kitchen. "That's going to be hard to work with. Can't we just wrap it up to support it or something."

"Don't worry, dear." Janet patted her thigh. "It will probably be fine with some rest. Of course, if it doesn't get any better by Friday, I would schedule a doctor's appointment. Do you want Lance to drive you home?"

"Oh no, I'll be fine. I sit in a booth most of the day. Someone will have to take over the tour, I guess. Let's pray it heals quickly." Piper shoved her fist to her cheek as she leaned against the counter beside her. "Thanks, Janet."

A muffled masculine whisper came from the baby monitor near the stove. "Hello, baby girl."

Janet called out, "Is she awake? Lance, bring her here—"

While Janet got pain medicine and water for Piper, Lance appeared with crutches in one hand and a sleepy Amelia cradled in his other arm. "I think I woke her with that squeaky utility door right next to her Pack 'n Play."

"Oh, I didn't think about that. The sitting room off that hallway has less light, and I didn't want to go up and down the stairs."

"Well, she doesn't seem too upset." Lance handed Piper the crutches with his eyes on Amelia.

Janet took the sleepy baby. "She's laid back. Doesn't mind being woken up because she gets all Grandma's attention," she cooed. "Isn't that right, Amelia?" The baby rubbed her nose in Janet's shoulder and let out a great big sigh.

"Be very happy, Amelia," Piper said as she stood up

with a crutch under each arm. "You don't have to walk around and risk spraining your ankle yet."

Janet and Lance laughed.

After Piper took some medicine offered by Janet, and persuaded both Hudsons that she did not need to go home, Lance opened the back door. "Come on, Miss Tour Guide. Those kids probably have corn coming out their ears, literally."

"Have you come up with any ideas for finishing the tour?" Piper waved a crutch in front of her.

"Yep." Lance grinned. "I think I have an idea."

# Chapter Six

Lance walked beside Piper as she hobbled through the grounds. Every once in a while, he'd catch himself reaching out when she seemed unsteady, but she was adamant about not needing help. If only he could forget the way she'd looked at him on the porch a few minutes ago. Putting all the words about gazebos and letters and spending time together into the present atmosphere was waking up old affection that was absolutely not welcome. He'd been rejected the first time when she'd reconciled with her ex-boyfriend. A swift lesson in unrequited first love. But an unanswered question pecked at Lance—why had she chosen Garrett over him?

Lance helped Piper sit in the back of the utility vehicle and laid her crutches on top of the passenger seat.

"Ah, my own carriage?" Piper jested.

"Good imagination." Lance waved over the teachers, who were helping kids tie their shoes after the romp in the corn pool. "Got your script?"

"Yes, sir." Piper waved it.

He got in the driver's seat, stretched out his white-knuckled fingers, then slung an elbow across the back of the seat to look over his shoulder. Piper faced away as she sat in the short bed, her hurt ankle rested on the green metal bed while her other foot was tucked under her thigh. When the group came up, she began to read her script while they followed the slow-moving vehicle.

"The Hudson family has farmed this land since the early 1900s. They were the first working farm in the area and the main supplier of eggs and produce to the Rapid Falls General Store, now known as Allie's Gas Station, on the east side of Rapid Falls." Piper projected her voice while the group stayed a good ten feet away from the moving vehicle. The teachers were extra cautious, walking backward so they could keep an eye on the kids, but the two women seemed to take great care to not repeat Piper's mishap.

The ground became a little bumpy right when Piper started talking about Grandpa Jo's first productive apple crop. She gripped the sides of the small bed and threw her voice over her shoulder. "Are you trying to knock me off?"

"Of course not." Lance faced forward and slowed to a crawl until they reached the storage shed. He allowed the vehicle to idle while the teachers took photos of the kids with the nursery rhyme cutouts. "How's your ankle?"

Piper scooted around and leaned up against the side of the bed instead of having her back to him. "It's very… throbby. Is that a word? But the painkillers Janet gave me are helping." She tilted her head to see from beneath the bill of her hat.

"The anti-inflammatory will kick in any minute." He shifted his attention to the metal building where he'd thought he'd be working most of the day.

"Hey, I appreciate you doing this. I know Sidney was concerned about staffing."

"It's my business, too, Piper."

She flushed and dropped her attention to her fidgeting fingers.

"Sorry. I didn't mean to talk down to you."

Piper only shrugged and dipped her chin in a not-worried-about-it kinda way.

"I just mean, even though I'd rather be on the production side of things, I am here to help out wherever I'm needed. Or should be, anyway." All of this land—this historic family farm—was worth the work. Piper's script had awakened some of his loyalty that had grown dormant while living in a different state. Lance was proud of his Hudson history. While Piper had read that history aloud, Lance knew it was exactly what he needed to hear. A positive reminder of where he came from and where he could go. It was as if Someone was using this change in plans for his own good. He huffed inwardly. His grandmother was speaking in his head, it seemed. God hadn't given Lance much of anything lately, and after the torment of a cheating wife and a failed marriage, how could he really trust that God was working in the simple, inconsequential activities of a family apple orchard?

The teachers led the kids up a hill to take photos next to the directional sign that showed arrows toward Rapid Falls, Des Moines, Minneapolis and Chicago.

"This might take a while." Lance sighed, put the vehicle into Park and threaded his leg across the bench seat beneath the crutches.

"I am so impressed with this place. All of it." Piper spoke almost breathlessly. "I didn't realize how much I missed being here. Turning my back on…on…all that was good… Well, it was a mistake I can hardly swallow."

Lance opened his mouth to speak but then thought better of it. If she knew it was good, then why did she turn her back on it? On him? He shouldn't even consider asking. They'd both suffered divorces and hardship. Now was a time of new beginnings.

Instead, he diverted the conversation away from Piper. "I thought I had it good in both Denver and Rapid Falls. Until I didn't."

"I am sorry about your ex," Piper said without any snark or humor. Purely genuine. Lance held back his accusation that Sidney shouldn't be talking to Piper about his private affairs. He couldn't get upset that Piper knew anything, or everything, about his situation. He'd moved back home without his wife, hadn't he? Of course people would talk and wonder.

The class began to swarm toward them again, so Lance nodded and turned back around, saying, "Looks like they are ready to continue."

"Yep." Piper scooted into her position facing the opposite direction, and once she gave a thumbs-up, he continued to drive.

After Piper shared about the Rapid Falls Harvest Festival and a few other events sponsored by the orchard, she gave a plug about the new pumpkin patch coming in October. Lance smiled, thinking of how excited his sister was to put into action something Lance had suggested. He breathed in the familiar scent of fresh grass and moisture in the air. Fall was a fantastic time of year around here.

As he pulled up next to the orchard booth, a crew member he'd hired for harvesting was taking care of customers. Lance shook his head. He'd hired the crew member for the Clyde's order. The guy looked uncomfortable helping young families instead of harvesting apples.

"Okay, folks. We're here." Piper began to grab her crutches. Lance swiftly took them and walked around to the back of the utility vehicle.

"Thanks." She held his hand to carefully climb out. "This wasn't too bad. I think they listened well, even so."

Lance kept his grip on her tiny fingers as she adjusted the crutches beneath her arms. "You did great, Piper. Grandpa Jo would be proud. On behalf of the Hudsons, thank you." Piper tilted her head and looked up at him with one eye closed to the sun directly overhead, seemingly confused. "What? Can't handle a compliment?"

She turned her focus on the orchard, and her glossy eyes made him question if she was getting emotional.

He shifted his weight and squeezed her hand gently. "Hey, Piper, are you okay?"

Quickly, she whipped her head to look at him straight on, releasing the scent of eucalyptus and citrus from her shampoo. "Guess our tour ends after they pick. I can get a ride back with your dad." A curt smile punctuated her matter-of-fact statement.

Lance dropped his hand from hers and crammed it in his pocket. "Sounds good. Take care of that ankle."

"I will. Thanks again, Lance."

She hobbled toward the class now lined up at the booth. The crew worker caught Lance's eye. "Hey, Mike. That's your replacement." He nodded in Piper's direction. "Want a ride?" Relief melted the tension on the young man's face.

Lance chuckled. When Mike hopped in next to him, Lance said, "Not your kind of work, huh?"

"I am no good with kids. Would rather pick apples all day."

"I get it. Don't worry. We're heading that way." Lance put the vehicle into Drive and turned around, catching a glimpse at Piper handing small baskets to the kids.

"That was like managing chaos." Mike whistled. "No, thank you."

Lance couldn't fully agree with Mike in a way. Kids weren't too bad. He'd wanted some of his own. The importance of family, young and old, was a consistent piece of Hudson history. Maybe that was why Lance had shoved aside telling his grandmother that his path toward having his own family had come to an abrupt dead end.

Lance and his crew spent the rest of the day picking fruit under a cloudless sky. By late afternoon, Lance had tossed aside his work polo, wearing only his white-T-shirt—once a necessary undergarment for his button-down pinstripes. He stepped off the ladder and rolled his aching neck, winced and stretched his arms up and across his torso.

He'd worked an office job for the past several years, and although it was in sales and production just like his job here at the orchard, this was an entirely different kind of brawn. Typing and phone calls did not require the tormented muscles that were now screaming for him to cease fire.

But no way would he stop. The pain was nothing compared to this forgotten feeling of a job well done. Sure, he'd excelled in his position back in Denver. But this kind of work was different. This was built into his Hudson genes. His hands had reached up and twisted apples off their branches in good, solid Hudson fashion.

Following in the careful, dedicated work of his dad and grandparents made the aches worth it.

When Lance opened the driver's door to the flatbed truck, his cell was vibrating on the dash. He answered after glancing at the number on the screen, "Hey, Tony. We've got a truck full of the best apples in Iowa." The wood bins behind him brimmed with the prettiest fruit this side of the Mississippi. Off in the distance, his crew was heading toward the parking lot. Maybe they were taking a break.

"That's great, Lance. I apologize for this, but the truck's schedule got messed up. It seems the only time that Clyde's can be in the area is first thing tomorrow. Is that going to work?"

"Uh…just a second." Lance pressed the phone to his shoulder. A couple of the guys were climbing into a pickup as if they were leaving. Mike lagged behind the rest of the crew, typing on his cell. "Hey, Mike!"

He turned around and called out, "What's up?"

"We've got a lot more work ahead. Tell your crew we'll feed them well, so they don't have to leave."

Mike opened his mouth to say something, glanced over at the crew, then jogged toward him. "Uh, Mr. Hudson, I think we have a misunderstanding."

Lance felt the weight of all those apples in the back of the truck resting on his sore shoulders. He held the phone to his ear. "Hey, Tony. Don't worry. We'll figure it out. I'll call back in a bit to get any details. Thanks." He ended the call.

Mike appeared antsy, looking down at his cell, then over his shoulder. His doe-eyed look at Lance reminded him of the children that Mike had so adamantly left behind at the orchard booth.

"What did we misunderstand? The temp agency

said you guys needed work. This is work. Since you have worked around here on and off in high school, we thought you were the best for the job."

"We need daytime work. All of us have been working as the night crew on a new I-80 exit ramp. Have an hour drive ahead of us." Mike's eyebrows tipped up in an apology. "Thought you knew when you called yesterday."

Lance shook his head. "Nope, I guess I missed that. Or the agency misunderstood my need." He crossed over the gravel path to Mike and held out a hand for a shake. "It's all good. You boys did a great job today. We'll see you tomorrow." They shook hands. Mike said goodbye, then swiveled and ran to the rest of the crew. He hopped in the bed of the truck, and they drove out of sight.

A sick feeling came over Lance as he drove toward the building. If there was one thing Lance had never done at his desk job, it was extending a deadline. If someone else was ready to take the next step, he was well trained to go the extra mile. Not only was it a good business tactic, but it was a way to let others know their value. He would decline or hesitate only if the risk was too great. And Lance was not unfamiliar with those instances. He had taken off many days during the darkest of his marital strife. He'd declined work conferences when Tara and he needed to spend time together. Lance was by no means a pushover at work, but he was not going to start off negotiating this new opportunity with Clyde's.

In the distance, the hayride was coming over the hill. Dad transported the last guests for the day. Piper's red hair was obvious as she sat in the very front of the trailer.

Lance parked the truck and met up with Sidney who was walking toward the hayride stop. "Hey, we've got our first order for Clyde's. We don't have any extra hands, and we need fifty boxes of our best apples. Clyde's is picking up at eight o'clock in the morning."

"Oh, wow. Two thousand apples? That's a lot to sort and pack. But I am sure Mom will help with Amelia."

They met up with Piper. Lance helped her down the steps with her crutches.

"So, Piper. Want to make some extra pay tonight?"

"Oh, how?" She boomeranged a look between the twins.

"We have a big order to fill. Might take us into the wee hours—" Lance rocked back on his heels.

"You can stay for dinner, like old times," Sidney exclaimed. Typical celebratory Sid.

But typical Piper wasn't standing before them. She nibbled on her lip and began to shake her head. "Oh, I don't think I can help. My…my…daughter needs me—"

"Sure, I get it." Lance nodded to Piper.

"Hey, kids." Dad walked up to them. "What's going on?" Lance explained what happened with the crew.

Dad hooked his thumbs on his belt. "Well, seems like the old Hudson work ethic will serve us well. Tonight's going to be like old times—a family affair." He turned to Piper. "Are you joining us?"

"She has to get back to her daughter," Sidney explained with a smile.

"Dad, you leave the heavy lifting to Sid and me." Lance would rather bear the burden of the order than have Dad risk hurting his back again.

Piper stepped back from the conversation between the siblings and their father so she could check her phone. She hadn't been able to get a signal to call her mom during the ride from the orchard, and she was nervous about a replay of forgetting Maelyn like a couple days ago.

Don headed toward the house, and Sidney rubbed Lance's arm, giving him a usual Sid pep talk. Piper leaned on a crutch and called her mom again. She plugged her ear with a finger as the field trip group swarmed the café patio to get a group picture.

Two rings, three… "Hey, Piper."

"Oh, hi, Mom. I was just calling to be sure all went…"

"Hi, Mom!" Maelyn's gleeful greeting in the background was Honeycrisp sweet.

"Hi, sweet girl! How was school?"

Mom answered, "She's in the back seat buckling up. Here, let me hand her the phone."

"Maelyn?"

"Mmm-hmm?"

"Hey, there. How was school?"

"It was good. Guess what?" Her lisp was adorable— one of those qualities that Piper didn't want her to grow out of too quickly. Just like when Maelyn used to say *compeeter* for *computer*. She'd grown out of that in first grade. Her lisp would disappear one day, so Piper would revel in every sweet lisped *s* until then. Stay away two-front teeth!

"What's up, buttercup?"

"Grandma's taking me to the trampoline park!"

"Really?" That was at least forty-five minutes away. Was Mom really up for the drive, the park, then figuring out dinner on the road? "That's great. Have so much fun. And be careful! Um… Can I talk to Grandma again?"

"Sure. Love you, Mom."

"I love you so much, Maelyn." She could hear the shuffling of the phone exchange between grandmother and granddaughter.

Mom said, "Hi, Piper," very enthusiastically. "Don't worry, we aren't driving yet. If only I had that Bluetooth thing. Hands-free would be nice so we can get a move on to Marion."

"Are you sure you want to go all that way? What about dinner?"

Mom laughed. "Well, they have these places called restaurants."

"Ha, ha. I know. But that's…that's expensive." And wasn't she trying to watch what she spent? Piper could probably count on one hand the number of restaurants she'd entered in the past eight years. "And you all won't get back 'til really close to bedtime."

"Piper Elaine Gray. Quit your worrying. This is what good grandmas do." She held a smile in her voice. Then she whispered, "Especially when they show up an hour late sometimes."

"That's really kind of you, but…" Piper's voice was a few octaves higher than her usual tone. Her throat squeezed with mixed emotion—thankful for Mom's redemptive gesture but miffed that she hadn't asked Piper first. Was this the best thing for Maelyn on a school night?

"And Bill is working near there, anyway, so he's going to meet us for dinner and ride back with us since his colleague drove. It's all planned out. You take the night off."

Piper glanced over at Sid and Lance. They were heading to the metal building. "Um, you know, they need extra help here. I might take the chance to earn some more hours and work late."

"Well, that's a good idea," Mom encouraged. "Don't you worry about us. We are going to have a grand ol' night."

Piper said goodnight to Maelyn, then ended the call. Sidney was gone, but Lance was lifting the garage door to the packaging area.

"Hey, Lance, do you all still need some extra help?"

The answer was written all over his face. Eyes wide with expectation, forehead wrinkled upward and a half smile that would surely double with her confirmation. "Are you available now?"

"I sure am." Piper shouldn't care about Lance's reaction, although she couldn't help but giggle when her prediction came true—a wide, flashing smile like she'd just given him a gift.

"You are a lifesaver, Piper. Don't think I could do it without you."

"Oh?" Piper's cheeks flushed. She focused on tucking the phone in her pocket, feeling foolish that those words had made her day. But it wasn't the first time he'd made her day in the past few hours. When he'd complimented her after their awkward tour in the utility vehicle, Lance couldn't have known what that meant to her.

He tilted his head like he was trying to lock his gaze with her downcast eyes. "We'll get started right away. Sidney's coming back after she checks on Amelia."

Piper nodded eagerly. "Sounds good. I've got the night off from parenting. So, I'm all yours." Again, she blushed. The heat wrapped around the nape of her neck, flaring up beneath her curls. This was ridiculous. She needed to rein in her overreactions to Lance's kind words. What practical thing could she say? "Um…will I get overtime for this?"

Lance chuckled. "Of course. You are an employee, aren't you?"

Yes. She was. Sidney's best friend and an employee. Nothing else, especially not to Lance Hudson, orchard manager and a simply encouraging guy who'd made her day—twice.

## Chapter Seven

The apple production team was really a family gathering, with Piper added for overwhelming need more than good measure. Don, Sidney, Lance and Piper worked on prepping the apples, while Janet began to situate the packaging materials. Amelia bounced in her Johnny Jump Up hanging from the office doorframe. Old eighties country music played on the radio. A few Hudsons would break into song every once in a while. Piper could not believe the simple work of cleaning and sorting apples would be so entertaining.

After a couple hours, Don pulled out a charcoal grill from a nearby shed and wheeled it over to the open garage door of the metal building.

"The corn's been frozen but will still taste like summer," Janet assured them while she, Sidney and Amelia headed to the house to grab some Iowa chops and sweet corn.

"It's been a long time since I've had sweet corn," Lance admitted as he stepped away from the apples to help his dad at the grill.

Piper opened her mouth to share how much Maelyn loves to help shuck, cook and especially eat sweet corn, but she stopped herself. Instead, she stretched her arms up and back, then walked off to admire the sunset and test her sore ankle. She gingerly stepped without a crutch to the big sycamore tree just at the edge of the dirt lane to the you-pick orchard. The sun neared the crest of the western hills, melting like strawberry sauce on an ice-cream sundae. Wispy clouds were painted a soft pink.

"I've always missed the Iowa sunsets." Lance joined her. "I had a photograph taken from this exact spot and made into a canvas. It's in my apartment—or, I mean, was. Guess it's in storage now." He breathed in...but never audibly breathed out.

Piper was sure she understood the tension coursing through Lance at the mention of what once was. "Are you going to get a place in Rapid Falls?"

"Eventually. I might think about doing some freelance work during the winter and look for a place between here and a bigger city—Waterloo or Marion."

Piper gave him the most playful look of surprise she could muster. "And miss out on Sidney's Winter Wonderland Light Show here?"

Lance stepped back and stared at her straight on. "Are you serious? Did she say that she was going to—"

"Uh-huh. I think it sounds delightful. But I am sure you don't."

"Well, the entertainment elements are profitable, I guess." Lance whistled. "As long as we can keep up the tradition of Hudson produce, too." He ran his hand over his short hair, then crossed his arms over his chest, staring in the direction of the sunset. "Have you been in Rapid Falls this whole time...you know...since high school?" His brows were cinched as if his question were almost painful to ask.

"Nope. Waterloo until a couple months ago." She bobbed her head, trying to find a question to divert the attention from her.

"I'll be honest. I was surprised at how quickly you got married. You and Garrett seemed like oil and water before your first breakup. We'd talked about it…that summer."

Whoa. Hairpin curve down memory lane was not where Piper had planned on heading this evening. She envied the sun's inevitable descent to a happy hiding place beyond the green hills to the west. "It was a quick decision. Seemed an easy one at the time." Sure, it had. She was pregnant and the father was off to a big future that brought his family so much pride.

The breeze rustled the leaves above. Piper shifted her gaze from the slipping sun to the sprawling tree branches. The usual pure-white bark was awash in a pink glow, the last remnants of light before nightfall.

"That was such a long time ago." She was thankful for the rosy shade blanketing everything right now. It was the second-best thing to nighttime. At least whatever red spread on her cheeks was masked. "I am sure Stanford was much more entertaining. But nothing can prepare you for washing thousands of apples to be eaten by Iowans everywhere." Her quick diversion from unwelcomed topics released some tension, and she leaned against the tree trunk.

Lance stared directly ahead. "Speaking of that, how long are you willing to stay tonight?"

Piper shrugged. "How long do you need me to stay?"

"I am thinking this is going to be an all-nighter kind of job. Got to get these all packaged and ready to go for pickup. Sid said she would make up the guest room for you."

"Ah, so you've already conspired with her. It used to be Sidney and me conspiring against you." She winked. Lance's features froze and he just held her gaze. Blue eyes sparkling in the cotton-candy light. A question seemed to crease the space between his eyebrows.

Piper gulped as discreetly as she could and braced herself. What did he want to ask?

Lance fought against the rising question that suddenly flooded his brain, pounding on his ears along with his beating pulse. Did she remember the time between his looking out for his sister and the day he left for Stanford? When the decision wasn't whether she'd say yes to her ex-boyfriend but whether she'd allow Lance to hold her hand when nobody else was looking? He couldn't believe his heart would do a one-eighty, and instead of suspecting Piper Gray as Sidney's partner in crime, he saw her for who she really was—this spunky beauty with a sense of humor that did him in.

But of course, looking back now, why wouldn't a guy have fallen for Piper? She was perfect "first love" material—until she wasn't. *He* hadn't been her first love, anyway. Now, Lance understood the hold that feeling could have on a person. It had shifted his perspective. Their breakup had had his heart stuck in idle for a long while. Until Tara had entered the picture. She was an Iowan living in California, just like him. And they seemed to have so much in common.

Second love was not much different—just a little more subtle, taking a little more time. Like watching the sun go from noon to dusk. From a sunny spark to a spectacular glow. Unfortunately, his marriage was like the afternoon light in a less-than-happy way—from a sure shine to completely dissolved.

Lance finally asked, "How's your ankle feeling?"

"Oh, it's better, I think." Piper looked down and wiggled her sneaker from side to side. "Just a slight twinge of pain. Hobbled over here without a crutch."

He nodded, stuffed his hands in his pockets and began to turn back.

"Wait!" Piper pointed to the sunset. "You'll miss it. It's as satisfying as witnessing the final surrender of a baby fighting sleep."

He tried to focus on the tiny sliver of light bubbling along the horizon, resisting the temptation to watch Piper. No. This woman could not compete with the sun. And Lance could not get all sentimental with old flames. He'd been burned enough.

Once the sun made its last bow from the painted sky, they both sighed in unison, and Lance continued back toward his dad. "Are you coming?"

Piper pushed away from the tree, winced and then began to walk, favoring her good ankle.

"Oh, hey. Let me help you." He offered his elbow. She threaded her arm through his, and just like earlier today, he escorted her, pushing away the annoying satisfaction of being needed.

He sighed once more.

Sidney and Mom were setting containers on the old picnic table outside the production area. A baby monitor lit up with an occasional sound from sleeping Amelia. Once the chops were ready, Dad said a blessing, and they dug in. Sitting in the cool fall evening, eating Iowa-grown food—well, Lance allowed himself to feel some peace at being home with those he loved. This was his favorite moment so far.

They chatted about Clyde's order and how they would handle the rest of the prep. Mostly, Sid, Piper and Lance would do the packaging. Dad just couldn't risk his back giving out again, and Mom had a volunteer shift at the retirement center.

Once they'd made a plan, and Piper texted her mom she'd spend the night, everyone had pretty much finished dinner and it was time to get to work. Sid explained the sorting machine to Piper while Lance began to unload the bushel bins.

"Just a sec." He jogged to the storage closet, pulling out an old stool. "Here you go, Piper. You probably shouldn't stand on that ankle for too long."

She just dipped her head and took her position. Strange. Instead of a simple thank-you, Piper seemed to stiffen as she took his offering.

"You feeling okay? Not used to the larger-than-life Piper-the-Great being so quiet."

"You are so thoughtful, Lance. That's all." She gave a small smile. "And… I am so full." She puffed her cheeks out and popped open her eyes.

Lance laughed. "How can I not give you a seat to keep your ankle comfortable for the night ahead?" He winked and patted his stomach. "And I am full, too. Dad is a grill master."

"And I am a professional corn-butterer!" Sidney called out as she gathered the flats of packaging materials.

This time, Piper managed a full-on grin.

They worked steadily toward the midnight hour. Lance would run from loading the apples to be cleaned and sorted to taking the ready boxes to the walk-in cooler. Piper inspected the clean apples for any bruises or markings that might be off-putting to customers.

They were fine to eat but would also go in the bin with the smaller apples. Sidney oversaw the final packaging.

More than once, Sidney would add to the bin of apples discarded for non-retail use. Lance nearly ran into her. "What's up, Sidney? Are you being a perfectionist tonight? We have a lot to package yet."

Piper swiveled on the stool. "Am I missing too many?"

Sidney laughed. "No, don't worry about it. It's always good to have a second pair of eyes."

Lance added, "You don't have to rush though. Just make sure you are catching any blemishes."

Piper's shoulders visibly sank, and she lowered her eyes to her bouncing knee. "Of course," she muttered and shook her head nervously. "I—I will do better."

Whoa. How had the feisty Piper Gray's confidence plummeted so suddenly?

"It's all good, Piper. We are a team." Lance reached his hand out to pat her shoulder, then thought better of it. This was work—a little suggestion shouldn't be a big deal.

She turned away, nodding. Sidney and Lance exchanged questioning glances, both shrugged, then continued with their work.

After another thirty minutes, Sidney sighed loudly and massaged her own shoulder. "Okay, Mr. Worker Bee. Let's take a break."

"We've hardly just begun," Lance huffed as he added more apples to the machine. "Can't you wait until we are halfway done?"

"You mean we aren't?" Piper exclaimed, casting an uneasy look between Sidney and Lance. "Uh..." She laughed half-heartedly. "Sorry. Just, wow, this is...a lot."

Lance shook away his fascination with Piper's obvious soft side. As much as her zest for life had clashed with Lance's careful ways growing up, he didn't necessarily like this shift in her demeanor. Sure, there was one thing about maturity calming a person, but shouldn't adulthood come with more confidence, not less?

Sidney stretched her arms above her head. "Well, you can keep working, but Mom's scotcheroos are calling my name."

Again, Piper looked back and forth between the siblings. Sidney challenged Lance with a playful hooked eyebrow and offered a mischievous grin to Piper. "Scotcheroo, Piper?"

"Ah, that's why we have always been friends," Piper chimed in. "You have a mom who has cultivated my taste for sugar." She caught Lance in her line of sight.

"I see how it is," he responded to her, laughing. "Once again, two against one. All I want to do is get this order done, and you two are sidetracked by chocolate and peanut butter. Go on."

Piper hopped off her stool and speed-walked with Sidney to the treats.

"Guess your ankle is all better!" Lance called out.

"Chocolate heals all things." Piper wiggled her foot. "Yup. All better."

She hadn't changed that much, Lance convinced himself as he shut down the machine and crossed over to join them. Although, he recalled Sidney being talked into the adventures of Piper Gray, whereas tonight, it was the other way around. Maybe he didn't realize his sister was an instigator for all things fun as much as Piper.

"Oh, how I've missed you," Piper declared to the peanut butter, Rice Krispies and thick chocolate ganache, then took a bite, her eyes fluttering shut. With a mouthful, she admitted, "Just how I remember."

"They are some of the best scotcheroos out there," Sidney added, licking her finger after finishing one off.

"I don't think I have had one since...since...our grad party?" Piper continued to eat.

"What? How can that be?" Sidney walked over to the utility sink and began to wash her hands. "It's an Iowa staple, almost as much as sweet corn."

Piper stepped back as Lance reached for a scotcheroo. She continued eating, not answering Sidney's question.

"Seriously, our grad party, Piper? Even I've had them since then...and I've lived in two different states." Lance savored the taste of his mom's baking.

Piper's eyes were wide, unenthusiastic, unemotional. Her entire expression was as if she were not fully here but transported to one of those other states. Lance nearly waved a hand in front of her face.

Cries in stereo—one from the baby monitor tucked in Sid's back pocket and the other muffled from behind the office door—broke Piper's frozen impression.

She turned away from Lance altogether. "Amelia's up! Can I get her? It's been so long since I've snuggled an infant." Sidney nodded, and Piper headed to the office door.

Whatever timidity laced her reactions tonight was chased away by her enthusiasm to help with the baby. Lance knew his niece could distract anyone from an unanswered question...or two.

# *Chapter Eight*

Piper was relieved to not be the center of attention as she picked up the baby. Of course, she wasn't really the center—those scotcheroos were unbelievable—but even Piper knew how odd she must seem. Not having a sweet treat that showed up at every Iowa function? Well, Piper hadn't been to any function outside her duplex while she'd been married. She may as well have been on an island all by her lonesome, with little Maelyn to keep her company, and Garrett showing up to remind her how insufficient she was as a housewife.

She kissed Amelia's dark head of hair. At least Garrett could never say she was an insufficient mother. If anything, he'd complained often that *the kid* got too much attention from her. She was fine with that, and in the end, she'd done exactly what she needed to do as a mother, first and foremost. A shudder went up her spine as she considered what might have happened if she hadn't…

Piper bounced a happy Amelia on her hip as she entered the production area. "This is the friendliest baby. She hardly knows me, and she's my new best friend." But she grimaced as Amelia grabbed a fistful of her red hair and tugged with a loud squeal.

"And it's almost midnight." Sidney rolled her eyes. "Always up for a party like her Auntie Piper." Sidney's voice caught Amelia's attention, and the baby girl immediately let go of Piper's hair and reached both hands out to her mama. Piper walked over to Sidney, who scooped up her baby.

"Babies are truly the only real sweetness in life." Piper's sentence transformed into baby talk as she tapped Amelia's nose. "Sometimes the only good thing, right?"

"They are," Sidney agreed but cast a worrisome look at Lance. He brushed her off with a shrug, then continued with his work. Did the guy not like kids at all? He wasn't thrilled about carting them on the hayride. But he was sweet with his niece. Maybe something had happened while Piper was in the office? Or maybe Piper appeared to be slacking, and they were holding back their disappointment in her work ethic. She glanced over at Lance again. A pressing wave of wonder overwhelmed her. Lance's expression of trying to push aside whatever bothered him was familiar. So familiar—Piper had seen the conflict often in her little girl. The resemblance was…uncanny.

She shook away the uncertainty of keeping her daughter away from Lance. But if she'd learned anything as an adult, it was that life didn't revolve around her. Protecting her daughter was absolutely the most important thing.

Sidney complained, "This baby seems very unaware of Mom's need for sleep." She planted a big kiss on Amelia's forehead, then grabbed her nursing cover and returned to the office to feed her.

Piper walked over to the machine where Lance was getting ready for the next shift.

"Okay, boss. I'll get back to work," Piper said, trying to shut down the voice telling her she was pretty much failing at this job and she should just go home. For the first couple hours, Piper hadn't been sure what she was looking for. They'd shown her the parts of the apples that had rubbed against the tree, creating a brown spot, but some weren't as obvious as others. And for Piper, she wasn't so picky about her fresh fruit. She'd have been thankful for this fruit on her own table.

Lance turned the machine on. "Just keep it up. We're right on schedule."

"If you call 11:52 p.m. an appropriate time to function around large equipment…" Piper's tone was thick with her usual sarcasm. These people did make her feel like herself more and more, even if she'd forgotten some days.

Lance laughed. "Well, I expect you would disagree with the schedule. I was getting worried that something was wrong earlier. You seemed like you were, well, timid—if that's even a familiar word to you."

Piper swallowed hard and began to pick up the apples on the large sorting tray. "It's familiar." And an understatement. She had been completely humbled by Lance's constant thoughtfulness. From the moment he'd offered her an arm when she'd twisted her ankle to the ride in the utility vehicle to the stool so she could sit when everyone else stood. "It's been a long day. And I guess a little intimidating to do this work for the first time ever."

"*Intimidating* is another word I wouldn't expect you to know."

Piper tossed a blemished apple in the nearby discard bin, feeling her anger rise. Another sign of fatigue, maybe. But she didn't like being under Lance's scrutiny. "I am sure your impression of me is far from accurate at this point in our lives. You saw the best of me in high school, you were gone for the worst, and now we are here, together, for the licking-our-wounds part."

"Our wounds?" Lance guffawed, but his brow dipped in hurt.

Piper softened her voice. "Let's face it. You know that I had a rough go, and I know that you've had a rough time. Honestly, I haven't had someone be as kind to me as you—and Sidney—in a long time. I so appreciate it, but it takes some getting used to when you've been cut down for so long."

"Piper, I don't know what you've gone through, but I didn't mean to criticize you—" Lance stepped away from his work. "You are still Piper-the-Great to all of us."

There he went again. Completely melting away Piper's usual guarded self. She muttered, "Thank you," then began to fumble with an apple.

Lance strode over and stood next to her. "Hey, I am sorry for my preconceived ideas. That's not fair to you."

What? This man heard her without an argument? Piper rubbed her chin, mainly to keep it from dropping. "Thank you."

"And I am sorry for whatever happened to you, Piper. As for me, it hurts like nothing I've felt before."

She sighed and slouched on her seat. "Only way to get through it is pray, I guess. Took way too long for me to learn that. But I had Maelyn to care for. Somehow God uses our love for another as a nudge…or a giant shove." These words tumbled out as the man held his mouth the same way as the little girl she'd tried to avoid mentioning did. Maelyn's father. No doubt. But the truth in this moment seemed important. Not the biological truth, but at least the leap of faith that had saved her.

"Prayer is great…when it's answered the way we

hope." Lance kicked his heel backward against the leg of the machine. "It's confusing when everything goes against what we thought to be true and prayers aren't answered the way we hope they'll be."

"Yeah, I know. It took me a year to realize that the answer I wanted was not the answer I needed."

"What did you want?"

*For Garrett to change.* Piper's face flooded red. How long had it been since she'd thought back on her effort to keep her marriage afloat? "Well, that part doesn't matter. But that marriage was not what I needed. God knows best." She breathed in and began to inspect some apples. "And I can't believe that He has me here, with you—you all—looking for slight blemishes in perfectly delicious apples." She laughed.

Lance only held amusement in his sparkling blue eyes. He didn't smile, but he wasn't frowning, either. He just watched her. Observing. She had shared more with Lance than any other person lately, and she had the proof of her past with him framed up in a perfect little girl. No blemish. There was no chance she would create any more scars in this during this new beginning, even if being surrounded by all that was graciously familiar encouraged her to share more than she should.

Lance had no need to correct Piper on her apple-sorting ability the rest of the night. She was unexpectedly lighter as they continued working, and he didn't want to disrupt that again. He was glad Piper had figured out how to cut off her own disappointment, but seemingly not unscathed. What had happened between her and Garrett? Something about her demeanor raised Lance's pulse, and not in a teenager-crush way, but in a protective way. He didn't like that Piper attributed her timidity to being criticized by Garrett, who'd caused more trouble for teachers than Piper and Sidney had ever really caused for Lance as a protective brother.

By three in the morning, they powered down the equipment, Sidney bundled up a sleeping Amelia and the four of them quietly headed to the house. Piper knew exactly where the guest room was. She stopped at the end of the hall and turned to them before they climbed the stairs. "Seems like old times," she whispered.

Sidney whispered back, "I left some pajamas and toiletries for you. Sleep tight."

Piper gave a thumbs-up and yawned as she disappeared into the guest room.

Lance crashed into his bed after brushing his teeth. As fatigue set in, something Piper said kept him from sleeping right away.

He couldn't decipher the difference between what he wanted and what he needed. And if he were honest, he'd never forgive his wife for derailing their plans for the future by chasing after her own wants. Piper spoke about faith giving her what she needed. But Lance refused to rely on a nudge from above to set him straight. His want for a family ached deep down. How could he turn his back on his longing for children? *He may not have much experience with kids but spending time with his niece proved that what Piper had said was true— they are the sweetest.*

Lance had to face the fact that fatherhood might not happen any time in the near future, even though he'd expected it to happen sooner than later while he was married.

Before he'd decided to take the job at the orchard, life had been as frustrating as bobbing for apples with a blindfold on. Slight misses were misses all the same.

If he thanked God for anything these days, it was the chance to make a difference where it mattered most. For his family.

He fell asleep after surrendering the last of his pent-up tension on a giant sigh only to wake up to Piper's charming laughter and the warming aroma of bacon and eggs.

Lance glanced at the clock. 7:02 a.m. Just a little more than three hours of sleep. Felt like five minutes.

Feeling a little more alive after showering, shaving and putting on fresh clothes, Lance bounded down the stairs. Today would be a great day, even if he was running on fumes. Their first big order was ready for pickup.

"Good morning, son," Dad greeted him as he placed a platter of eggs and bacon on the table. Sidney was feeding Amelia oatmeal at her high chair, and Mom and Piper were chatting in the kitchen.

"It's a great morning. Our order to Clyde's is ready to go." He lowered into a seat at the dining table. Piper joined them at the table, cradling a mug. Had she gotten more sleep than he had? Her face was bright, and her curls showed no sign of bedhead. The red hair bounced just a little off her shoulders. She wore a clean orchard uniform shirt and sipped her coffee.

"I need one of those." Lance nodded at Piper's mug.

"It's. So. Good." Piper exaggerated each word, then narrowed her eyes at Lance with a devious smile.

Lance chuckled and rolled his eyes. It almost seemed like Piper had never missed a breakfast in this house. She seemed as comfortable as any family member would be, regardless of time passing. He was impressed they could easily reconnect with Piper despite being apart for so long.

"Here you go." Mom filled up the empty mug at Lance's place setting. "Don't let Piper get to you, son. She's just jealous you got a little more sleep than she did." Lance looked up at Mom to catch her wink at Piper.

Piper gave a pretend pout before putting the mug to her lips and smiling as she sipped.

Breakfast this morning was like finding a hidden apple after thinking harvest was over. The warmth of his family, the buttery homemade biscuits and the comfort of home were once indulgences of the past, but the feeling was sustained even after all his growing up. He even allowed himself to laugh with everyone at Piper's snark and banter with Sidney. Lance sank into his seat, perfectly content by the last sip of coffee and the final bite of eggs.

As they finished up, the front door opened and closed. Everyone paused.

"Don? Janet?" Nonny's voice rang through the house, and Dad sprung to his feet, heading to the foyer.

Lance exchanged an uneasy look with Mom, and she got up and patted his hand. "You've got this, son." She grabbed the coffeepot and headed into the kitchen.

Nonny was on Dad's arm as she entered the room. "I can't believe my grandson has been here for a week and hasn't come to visit me. So, I came myself." Lance stood. "There he is!" she exclaimed, then clapped her hands and held them out.

Lance wrapped her in a hug. She was tiny and fragile. "Hello, Nonny."

She patted his cheek. "As handsome as ever. But without your bride?"

Dad jumped in and said, "Mother, Janet's making some more coffee." He, Piper and Sid began to clear the table. Nonny's best friend's funeral had happened in the thick of Lance finalizing the divorce, so everyone had agreed to allow him to tell Nonny in person. And Lance felt it was only right to return the heirloom engagement ring, too.

Lance helped Nonny take a seat. "I've been meaning to come by, but you know how opening week is."

"I do." She splayed her hands on the table. "I didn't see you at Bea's funeral, either." She wagged her head. "Work can be a distraction, you know?"

He lowered into the seat next to her and squeezed her hand.

Piper reached over to take his plate and empty mug.

"Piper's here?" Nonny reached for Piper's hand, and Piper took it and greeted her. "Haven't seen you in ages, dear. You practically took up residence here when you were younger." She gargled a laugh.

Piper rounded her eyes, and her tight lips activated a dimple. "Now your grandson had us work 'til almost four o'clock this morning. Can you believe it?"

Lance playfully glared at her but bit his lip to avoid a grin. He turned to Nonny. "We got a big order finished."

"Better than getting in trouble at that time," Nonny chuckled. "Oh, Piper. I know times were hard for you back then. Don and Janet loved helping you out."

"They're the best," Piper affirmed, then swiveled away with the plates.

Nonny suggested, "Lance, let's catch up on the porch. It's a beautiful morning."

"Sounds good." Lance scooted back and helped Nonny to her feet. Mom followed them outside with a tray of coffee and mugs. When they got to the porch, Nonny crossed to one of the rocking chairs.

"Here, let me help—" Lance reached out to assist her. The petite woman planted her fist on her hip like she would when he was a little boy under her watch. But instead of the stern look of reprimand for climbing trees at the cost of his chores, Nonny just stared, waiting. And he was pretty sure it wasn't for his assistance.

"Er...everything okay?" His voice was scratchy.

"You tell me."

"I have been meaning to talk with you, Nonny."

"You are here alone. Not wearing your wedding ring. What's going on, Lance?"

"Let's sit down." He motioned to the rockers. "Nonny, there is something I have to tell you."

## Chapter Nine

Piper hurried down the hallway to grab her hat from her room. She was full and sleepy, but a whole day of work lay ahead. The Hudsons had completely distracted her from calling Maelyn this morning to make sure all was well. Last night, Mom had texted just before she tucked Maelyn in, and Piper was able to confirm she was staying here. But still, she longed to hear Maelyn's sweet voice. She had never spent the night away from her before.

Piper put on her hat, checking herself in the mirror. The room behind her was from a dream, it seemed—a past calm before the storm—and life as a teen under Mom's roof hadn't necessarily been calm. But under the Hudson roof, it had been. The pink-and-ivory damask quilt on the bed behind her had once been used for a fort in the living room, much to Janet's chagrin. This room had been referred to as "Piper's room" that summer when she'd stayed for three weeks while Mom sorted through her late mother's affairs down in Des Moines. The mirror framed this time capsule behind her, and at first glance, she hadn't really changed, either. Same oval shape face, hardly faded dusting of freckles and the same four-dollar mascara on her lashes.

Funny how even Nonny remembered Piper of yesteryear—needing a place because times were hard back then. Piper had been one of those bruised apples turned inside out. All banged up on the inside, with hardly a blemish on the outside. Now, she had just completed her first week of working. All those banged up feelings she'd admitted to Lance last night were fading fast in this place she adored. The work left her feeling accomplished after the disaster that was her marriage followed her less-than-ideal childhood with her mother and stepfather.

"You can do this," she said to her reflection. "Piper-the-Great, part two."

She rushed down the hall, ignoring the twinge of pain in her ankle. Her contemplative moment might just cost her the perfect record of star employee she was trying to cultivate. Turning the corner, Piper slammed hat-bill first into Lance's massive chest. Her hat popped off, Lance caught it and she gripped his arms to steady herself.

"Whoa, I'm sorry." Piper stepped back and ran her fingers through her hair, ignoring the promised strength of his muscular arms.

"Didn't see you coming. Are you okay?" His gaze darted around her face and hair. He brushed back a loose curl across her cheek, his other hand holding her hat to his chest. "You have a red mark." He ran his thumb over her forehead. Goosebumps rose on her arms. Lance switched gears from all business manager to all careful giant. His voice was soft, and each movement was gentle, subtle. So unlike his broad, statuesque appearance. Piper used to think Janet's nickname for him, Teddy Bear, was childish—until she and Lance had become better friends their senior year. He had always been a strong pillar for his sister. But that summer, Lance had offered Piper his strength as a refuge. And she was ever thankful for that.

"It doesn't hurt." She took the hat from his hand and crammed it on, covering most of her forehead. "See. No one will notice, either."

His Adam's apple bobbed against his polo shirt. "Well, we are going to be late. I have to get something for my grandmother." His jaw twitched under his clean-shaven skin. "Do you think you can wait for the delivery truck? I'll be there as soon as I can. I just have to get this done."

"Sure. I will wait. I don't have to be up at the orchard 'til nine."

"Thanks." He wore a faraway look.

She reached out and placed her hand on his arm again. "You okay, Lance?"

"Not really." He breathed in. "Had to share about my divorce with Nonny. Last to know."

"Oh, I'm sorry." She'd wondered about that when Nonny had asked about his bride.

"It's tough disappointing those you love." His nostrils flared. "She thought the world of Tara. I didn't have the heart to tell her why we broke up."

Piper recalled Sid sharing that the reason was infidelity. She wasn't going to pretend not to know—especially since her acting oblivious would only make Lance have to speak it aloud. She wouldn't put him through that. She knew how hard admission could be. "Did Nonny ask what happened?"

He shook his head.

"Sometimes you just share things on an as-needed basis, you know? I find that's the best." She sighed. "One day, it might be appropriate to share. But during the thick of the pain, it's like removing the Band-Aid before the bleeding's stopped. At least, that's a good analogy for a second grader." She bit her lip and adjusted the hat.

Lance's chin dimpled. "How is your daughter handling the divorce?"

"She's good. Kids are resilient, you know." Her words were shaky. "Let's just say that her life became ten times better when we left." Piper inhaled so deeply that the cedar-and-mint scent of Lance's aftershave overwhelmed her senses. Good—she had a very bitter taste on her tongue. "You should do what's right for you at this point, Lance. Don't give more than you have, you know? Need-to-know basis is enough."

"I left her on the porch while she was trying to refuse to take back her ring." He hung his head like a disappointed child.

Piper reached up to run her hand along his hairline instinctually. She paused. His blue eyes searched her face expectantly. "I—I am sorry. I know how close you and Nonny are."

He took her hand and threaded their fingers together, resting them on his chest. "Thanks, Piper. Seems like you have just the right advice. I remember that about you."

"You do? We had some great conversations back then." She fell into his gaze for one, two, three heartbeats, then caught herself and slid her hand away. "I'd better go wait for that truck."

He dipped his chin and headed upstairs.

Lance was undoubtedly Maelyn's father. In so many

ways. From his expressions to the round shape of his face. And even more obvious, the caring, gentle giant was so much like her lovebug daughter who would snake a tiny arm around her mother's neck when Piper would give into tears on the loneliest nights. "There, there, Mama, don't cry." Maelyn's little fingers would thrum on her shoulder. Her sweet voice would hitch when she'd say, "Are you okay?"

Of course, she was no doubt imitating Piper's own nurturing. But after Piper parted ways with Lance this morning, she suspected that Hudson DNA had shaped much of her daughter's natural compassion. As she walked to the delivery truck, she looked over at Lance's grandmother waiting on the porch for her brokenhearted grandson. An agonizing suspicion rose in her chest—keeping Maelyn away from this family was doing more harm than good. Lance Hudson would never deny his daughter the love she deserved.

How wide and deep would that compassion be for a woman whose philosophy about a need-to-know basis had betrayed Lance, the teddy bear?

After heading up to his room and fishing out the ring box from his still-unpacked toiletry bag, Lance raced downstairs with a little more confidence. Speaking with Piper had been a nice buffer between Nonny's shock and giving the ring back. Meeting someone who was traversing this same post-divorce path gave him an anchor of peace. Not that Piper had made him feel better about his situation, but she'd reminded him to move at his own pace—a slow crawl that wasn't his typical mode. Lance pushed open the porch door just as the Clyde's delivery truck pulled into the orchard parking lot in the distance.

Nonny stopped rocking and held up her hand. "Look here, Lance. I gave you that ring, and that's that. Whatever happened between you and Tara—well, that's just such an unexpected grief. But I don't want the ring back. Just like I give you my love no matter what happens. No conditions, you hear?"

Her words tried to convince his heart. Besides the order for Clyde's, there was nothing else in the world that he wanted to finalize. "Nonny. I need you to have it. I... I...need to move forward."

"How is returning a family heirloom moving forward?" Nonny pushed herself to her feet. "Son, you have a whole lot of life to live. That ring is for whatever that life ahead might bring. It's not going to do any good sitting in my dresser drawer back at the retirement community." She gingerly walked toward him. Her head was tilted back like she was inspecting the porch roof. Lance had forgotten how little his Nonny was.

Only in stature. Her spirit encapsulated the entirety of Hudson loyalty.

"You are one of the most important souls in my life. I am sad for what you went through, but I am glad to know how much you have to look forward to. Boosting our family legacy?" She beamed. "Now, we've got to start praying for discernment for whose finger that ring really belongs on." She covered the ring box with her thin fingers, lifted it from his hand, then tucked it in his shirt pocket. "I'll also pray for you. Whatever happened between you two—" She clicked her tongue and shook her head. "Well, it's still gotta hurt." Nonny examined his face, her eyes bubbling with moisture. "I'm so sorry, Lance," she whispered.

He pushed aside the building desire to point all fingers at Tara in response. But that would do nobody any good. Choices had been made. And papers signed.

The love his grandmother declared for him just now hadn't been present in his own heart in quite some time. Tara even admitted she'd never really felt that way for him, ever.

What had she said?

*I enjoyed our friendship, and our tie to Iowa. But were we ever truly in love?*

Lance squeezed Nonny's hand and offered his elbow to escort her to the car, trying to keep words bottled deep down. Nonny was the person who'd first taught him *if you can't say anything nice...*

And recalling the last words with Tara brought up all sorts of not-nice things. Especially because Lance had thought he *was* in love—the whole time. He couldn't trust himself to know. Both times he'd been left with heartache.

He noticed Piper talking to the driver outside the metal building. She waved at Lance, and the driver turned and dipped his hat. Lance held up a finger to signal he'd be right with them, then opened the driver's door for Nonny.

"Thank you, dear." She patted his cheek and lowered into the seat. "I might be small, but I feel like a twenty-year-old behind the wheel." She gave a devious grin.

"Be careful."

"You, too." She lifted a finger and jabbed him in the chest. "Right here. You've got time."

Nonny drove away, and Lance felt a little lighter. Except for the ring box in his pocket. But Nonny was right—a family heirloom was something to hang on to. More and more, Lance was growing further from the last woman who wore the ring, and more at peace with walking this new path toward—

Piper appeared at the end of the sidewalk. He chuckled and rolled his eyes at himself, focusing on Clyde's truck instead.

## Chapter Ten

Lance spent the next few days in constant production mode. It'd been nice focusing on work and moving further and further away from that heartbreaking moment with Nonny. He took advantage of the hired crew during the daytime hours. They continued to harvest the apples and package them for storage. Clyde's was set to come back, and this time, Lance would try to not forfeit sleep to get the order finished. But he resisted reflecting back on that twenty-four-hour period spent with Piper, the woman who'd seemed to have been part of his family's life all along. Curiosity pricked him every time he glimpsed her when she didn't know anyone was watching. Weariness held fast to her brow and tugged at her mouth's corners in between the bright smiles and snarky teasing.

Lance couldn't help but wonder what might have been if he'd put up a fight to win Piper over when Garrett had shown up. Would they both be here on the other side of failed marriages, or would they be together—

Lance took a deep breath to ground him in reality. What-ifs were not the need-to-knows he should spend his thinking time on. He left the crisp, cool morning and stepped inside the warm café. Immediately, his stomach growled at the warm scent of freshly baked apples, a hint of cinnamon and rich buttery goodness. Four quaint tables were set with red-and-white-checkered tablecloths and a café menu on a stand. The last time he'd visited Iowa, he had been surprised at how quickly this little building had come together. What had once been a small garage for all the work vehicles had been transformed into an idyllic orchard café with red siding and white trim on the outside, and on the inside, the very best part—shelves lined with applesauce, apple butter and packaged treats. A bakery case filled with fresh apple pastries and pies separated the dining area from the kitchen entrance.

"Good morning, Marge," Lance greeted her loudly. He spied the café manager pulling out fresh muffins from the industrial oven in the back.

"It's a beautiful morning, isn't it?" Her smile dazzled through the steam of the hot tray she carried with oven mitts that matched the tablecloths. Marge's cheery disposition fit this place perfectly. Dancing blue eyes, perfectly curled and coifed colored blond hair and rosy cheeks. Her age was given away only in the wrinkles around her eyes and mouth. Smiling wrinkles. Joyful aging. Mom always said that she had a hard time believing that her godmother, Marge, was a young adult when Mom was born.

"I'll take an apple fritter and a refill on this." He held up his cup.

"Your usual?" She raised a brow with amusement. Lance nodded, and Marge discarded her oven mitts to fill his order.

A text from a coworker back in Denver popped up on his phone.

Saw that Tara got married yesterday. Man, it's been too long since we talked.

Lance groaned.

"Everything okay?" Piper joined him at the glass display case.

"Oh, hey." He shifted his weight from one foot to the other. Heat wormed around his chest. Last time he'd found out the woman he had been in love with was married—well, it had been Piper. "Um…yes, everything's fine."

Piper seemed to take his word for it. "That's good. My weakness has quickly become Marge's apple fritters. Maelyn will be excited that I left one for her when she wakes up. School's out today. It's a workday for the teachers—" She paused and bit her lip. "And there I go, rattling on." She rolled her eyes and pursed her lips. Lance just looked away. No added sweetness needed for his breakfast. "Anyway, I said I would bring some to church on Sunday." She leaned an elbow on the top of the display case as Marge filled Lance's coffee mug to the brim. "Do you think I could pay for a dozen now, Marge? I can pick them up at the end of the day."

"Of course, dear. Good thing you caught me before we open. Those are always the first to go."

"Imagine that? An apple orchard selling out of appley things." Piper giggled. Marge winked, obviously accustomed to Piper's humor.

"You and Lance have been making me work hard in that kitchen. I think fritter production is up by two hundred percent."

Piper and Lance exchanged surprised glances, then laughed.

# Loyal Readers
# FREE BOOKS Voucher

## We're giving away THOUSANDS of FREE BOOKS

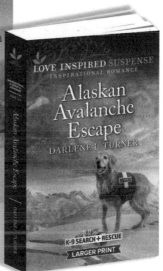

# Get up to 4 FREE FABULOUS BOOKS You Love!

To thank you for being a loyal reader we'd like to send you up to 4 FREE BOOKS, absolutely free when you try the Harlequin Reader Service.

Just write "YES" on the Loyal Reader Voucher and we'll send you 2 free books from each series you choose and a Free Mystery Gift, altogether worth over $20.

Try **Love Inspired® Romance Larger-Print** and get 2 books and fall in love with inspirational romances that take you on an uplifting journey of faith, forgiveness and hope.

Try **Love Inspired® Suspense Larger-Print** and get 2 books where courage and optimism unite in stories of faith and love in the face of danger.

Or **TRY BOTH** and get 2 books from each series!

Your free books are completely free, even the shipping! If you continue with your subscription, you can look forward to curated monthly shipments of brand-new books from your selected series, always at a discount off the cover price! Plus you can cancel any time.

So don't miss out, return your Loyal Readers Voucher today to get your Free books.

*Pam Powers*

# LOYAL READER
# FREE BOOKS VOUCHER

**YES! I Love Reading, please send me up to 4 FREE BOOKS and a Free Mystery Gift from the series I select.**

Just write in "YES" on the dotted line below then return this card today and we'll send your free books & gift asap!

➡ ─ ─ YES ─ ─ ⬅

Which do you prefer?

☐ **Love Inspired®
Romance
Larger-Print**
122/322 IDL GRCU

☐ **Love Inspired®
Suspense
Larger-Print**
107/307 IDL GRCU

☐ **BOTH**
122/322 & 107/307
IDL GRDJ

FIRST NAME

LAST NAME

ADDRESS

APT.#

CITY

STATE/PROV.

ZIP/POSTAL CODE

EMAIL ☐ Please check this box if you would like to receive newsletters and promotional emails from Harlequin Enterprises ULC and its affiliates. You can unsubscribe anytime.

LI/LIS-622-LR_MMM22

"Can't stay away from near perfection," Piper teased with an elbow nudge to his arm.

And for a brief second, Lance's mind slipped to a response that was less in jest and more flirtatious than he would ever allow. He'd once thought Piper came pretty close to perfection itself. How wrong he'd been, thinking she could be the one for him when the feeling wasn't mutual.

"Guess it's time to get to work." Piper slipped past him while he held open the door to the outside sitting area.

"Yep. Lots to do."

Before going their separate directions, Piper gave him a questioning look. "Um, do you need any help with production, preferably after hours?"

"Do you know someone?"

She pushed her shoulder up to her cheek and gave the most adorable grin. "Yours truly. Trying to help with some of Mom's bills."

"Ah, I see. There's another order coming up. I'll figure out what the hours might look like."

"Great. Thanks, Lance." Piper opened her mouth as if to speak again, but instead, she just nodded and headed to the hayride station.

"Hey, brother." Sidney approached as a group of customers dispersed from the admission door. "Another day in paradise." She smiled. Had she been listening to their conversation? Or reading Lance's mind? Paradise, perfection… What was the deal with all the *p* words today? "Think you can join me at the pumpkin patch to finalize plans?"

Lance chuckled at the additional alliteration. "Sure. I was down there the other day. Looks like a good crop."

"Yes, it's going to be so much fun for the families."

Lance laughed. "Fun is your middle name, Sid."

"You know it. Hey, is that—" Sidney stepped down the path. "Karen!" she hollered. "It's Piper's mom," Sidney squealed. "And Maelyn!" She jogged over to the woman and little girl who now walked toward them.

Wow, Piper's mom had hardly changed at all. And the little girl? Well, there wasn't any question that she was Piper's daughter.

In the distance, Lance saw Piper standing on the top step of the hayride. She yanked her hat off her head, shaded her eyes with her hands, then ran down the steps toward them.

Piper raced down the path. Life and work were suddenly colliding like two bushel bins crashing together and spilling produce all over. She'd thought she had dodged this kind of incident when Maelyn's therapy appointment had landed on the same day as her field trip last week. What were they doing here? Mom hadn't mention anything about this. All her mom had talked about these past couple days was needing extra shifts for bills—a hint to Piper, also.

Now, Mom had Lance's attention. Her typical hand gestures flailed about while she spoke, and Lance seemed a perfect gentleman, listening without a flicker of interest beyond Mom's gaze.

Piper slowed from a jog to a fast walk as she approached, trying to calm herself so her voice wouldn't come out in a stressed high pitch. The vein pulsing in her forehead was the usual indication that whatever sound she made would rival a dolphin's screech.

Sidney bent over with her hands on her knees, beaming at Maelyn. "Last time I saw you, I surprised your mom in Waterloo. You were hiding behind your mama's legs while we chatted on the porch. You weren't even knee-high. Now look at you!"

Maelyn offered a big toothless grin and rocked on her heels like she would when she was nervous in a school program. She reached her hand out to her grandma, who didn't seem to notice.

"Maelyn, this was your mother's best friend all growing up," Mom said, placing her hand on Maelyn's shoulder. *Better than nothing at all,* Piper thought.

Piper's voice cracked as she announced, "Hey, Mae. Mama's here." Everyone turned to her. She didn't look at anyone in the eye except her little girl. She reached out and embraced the hand that was desperate for a secure grasp.

Maelyn squealed and wrapped her arms around Piper's waist. "Mommy! Surprise!" She tossed her head back and gave the biggest grin beneath an upturned nose. "Grandma said we could come here instead of watching cartoons on my day off."

"Oh, really?" Piper managed an uncomplicated grin at her mom, although all the knots inside her were very complex. "You should have mentioned it, Mom."

Piper was holding her little girl while Maelyn's unknowing daddy loomed just beyond the long, braided pigtails snaking down her overalls.

Sidney straightened and crossed her arms atop her uniform shirt. "Don't worry, Piper. I have some time today. I'll head over to the orchard booth and help any customers. You all check out the corn pool then ride together on the hayride. You can relieve me then." Sidney to the rescue.

"Good idea. Thanks, Sid. Come on. Let's go find some corn." Piper quickly snagged Maelyn's hand and walked away.

"Slow down, Piper," Mom stuttered on a laugh. "You are ready to go, aren't you?"

"I don't want Sidney waiting too long," Piper explained as Mom came up beside her. She turned her head away from Maelyn to her left and whispered to Mom on her right, "I am honestly shocked."

"I am honestly overwhelmed." Her mother surrendered a desperate look. "Piper, let's just have fun. You and I will talk when Sidney can entertain Maelyn."

Entertain Maelyn? Piper sighed, trying to ward off a defensive remark at the audacity of Mom relying on Sidney to care for Piper's child. Piper relied on Mom *alone*. Maybe it shouldn't be a one-way street, but Piper would not allow anything to jeopardize Maelyn's security. And while Piper would trust Sidney to take care of Maelyn in a heartbeat, Piper didn't trust that questions wouldn't arise when one twin stared into the face of another twin's child for any prolonged length of time.

"Oh, the corn pool is huge!" Maelyn jumped up and down, yanking Piper's arm.

The corn pool sprawled the length of a tennis court, according to the tour script that Piper had recited from the back of the utility vehicle when she'd hurt her ankle. She thought about how Lance had mentioned he'd hardly been around kids, yet he was super sweet with his niece. Could Piper trust that he would be anything close to a good dad, or even a willing participant in Maelyn's life? At this point, after the disastrous past one, Piper knew that no dad at all was better than a disappointing father figure. Maelyn didn't need one more man in her life treating her like a shadow.

Mostly, Piper dreaded the response from the whole Hudson family if this secret were to get out. The biggest secret of Lance's life.

She just couldn't let him find out. Not when so much heartache had already been felt.

As usual, Maelyn observed the other kids playing before venturing in herself. She splayed her hands on the wooden edge and leaned forward, as if peering into water and not a gazillion corn kernels.

"Go on, Maelyn. Take off your shoes and hop in." Piper's mom sat on the edge next to her and peered into her granddaughter's face. "It's not deep."

Piper knelt beside Maelyn, certain that her little girl wasn't worried about the corn. She was assessing the rambunctious boys dumping kernels on each other's heads and the two little girls burying their legs in the yellow bits. Maelyn stared hard at the corn beneath her only when one of the other children looked their way.

Piper understood. She snaked her hand around Maelyn's waist. "Want me to go in with you?"

Maelyn's eyes rounded. She fiercely nodded.

"Of course, sweet girl." Piper pushed off her sneakers at the heels and swung her legs around, allowing her feet to sink into the corn. "Oh, what a strange feeling. It's like being inside a bean bag." She laughed and held out her hands to Maelyn. "Come on, Mae."

Maelyn bit her lip, then slowly pushed off her slip-on canvas shoes and propped her knees up on the edge.

Piper's mom plopped down next to Maelyn. "If your grandma can get in, Maelyn, then you can, too. Watch me." Mom tapped Maelyn's nose and plunged her socked feet in. "See, Grandma's as cool as your mama." She chuckled and held out her hand to Maelyn. The signature crease of worry between Mom's brows appeared, just like it did whenever she witnessed Maelyn's usual hesitation about kid-friendly activities. Piper winced at the missed opportunities for her daughter to bloom. Those times when Maelyn couldn't attend events like kindergarten roundup or school ice-cream socials. All because Garrett had refused to drive them, and Piper had had nobody else to ask until Sue had moved in next door.

Maelyn slowly allowed her feet to sink into the pool.

"There you go." Mom cheered. "See, isn't it fun?"

Maelyn's cute little nose scrunched up and pushed all her freckles into folds. "It's so weird."

Piper released all sorts of pent-up air and said an inaudible prayer of thanks for Mom's way of encouraging her daughter without shame.

They played for several minutes. Maelyn wanted her legs buried like they were in sand at the beach, and Mom took pictures with her phone. Piper noticed Lance driving a flatbed truck to the back orchard, waving in the direction of the hayride station, although Piper couldn't see the station from her angle.

"I think the hayride is back from its first round. We should head over to the orchard." Mom and Piper took each of Maelyn's hands, and they all stomped their way out of the pool. While they put on their shoes, they also dug out kernels of corn lodged in their socks. And as they walked over to the hayride, they stopped a couple times as Mom and then Maelyn had to fish out a kernel that had slipped to the bottom of their feet.

The hayride was pleasant, except for Mom slipping her readers on and being consumed with her phone for most of the ride. That worry line kept digging deeper. Once they got to the orchard booth, Sidney handed Maelyn and Mom two baskets, and Piper walked them to the gate, explaining the lay of the land.

"Okay, you're all set. How about you all fill your baskets and then we can have lunch? I get a thirty-minute break around noon."

"Sounds good."

Maelyn ran up to the first tree and peered up into the branches. Piper placed a hand on Mom's arm. "You seem preoccupied. What's going on?"

Mom searched Piper's eyes. "I can't keep doing this, Piper."

"Doing what?"

"Watching Maelyn. Work is putting the pressure on. They need me to fill the afternoon shift. I'd be a fool to turn down the chance at extra pay...what with—"

"You came here to tell me you can't watch my daughter anymore?" Piper's voice climbed octaves. "I mean, you came to my *work* to tell me—" Piper may as well have had an apple lodged in her throat.

"Let's talk at lunch. We'll figure it out." Mom started to walk toward Maelyn. "But, Piper, this was just an interim thing, right?" She glanced at the booth and the rows of trees. "Surely, you've been thinking beyond a seasonal temp job?"

Piper's face heated as she considered how she hadn't thought once about that. Mom turned and helped Maelyn climb a step stool. Hudson Orchard had been exactly what she needed. She'd harvested some joy and comfort here. Now what?

For the rest of the morning, Piper was only half listening as customers asked questions, and she was slow to respond more than once. What would she do if Maelyn didn't have someone at home after school? Suddenly, sitting in this booth seemed highly inadequate for this new life Piper was trying to create. The open-air wooden structure was strangely closing in on her on all sides.

## Chapter Eleven

When they found a table at lunch, Mom dug right back in to their conversation from earlier. "I think you should consider working as an associate in the schools. It would give you consistent hours and decent insurance." She peered down at Maelyn, who was focused on dipping her chicken nuggets in ketchup. "And the same schedule as Maelyn."

"Wow, Mom. You've already looked into it for me?" Piper's throat tightened. "I don't know about working in Rapid Falls CSD."

"Any other kind of job will probably require daycare." Mom leaned over and turned her head away from Maelyn. "I've looked into that for you, too."

"I'd probably be working to cover daycare costs." Piper glanced at Maelyn who was paying attention to other customers. "Mom, we just need some more time. You saw how the corn pool went. She's still adjusting."

"She'll be fine," Mom half whispered. "You don't think I know what it's like to care for a child as a single parent? Life doesn't wait for you to be ready."

Piper ogled at the woman who'd been emotionally absent for most of Piper's childhood. Of course, Piper blamed her stepdad for the most part. Had Mom been trying to survive, not realizing it was at her daughter's expense? "I want more for Maelyn. She deserves a thriving childhood."

"What are you saying? You didn't have that?"

Piper shrugged. "I am just saying that Maelyn comes first."

"You make me sound like a horrible grandmother."

"Mom, you have been great." Piper sighed. "It's a delicate situation." Mom's confused look wasn't surprising. *Delicate* wasn't a word in the Gray vocabulary. Big emotions were tamed with doing the next practical thing. Plastering on a smile and making dinner. Or running away to a happier place. Piper looked around the orchard. This place—

"Where's Maelyn?" She swiveled in her seat. Her daughter was gone.

After a quick bite at home, Lance headed to check on the production crew. The little café was buzzing with customers and the corn pool swarmed with kids. A day off for Rapid Falls Community School District meant lots of business for Hudson Orchard.

The crew was making progress. He inspected the packaged apples in the storage cooler, pleased with the pacing they'd set. When he left the frigid air, Mike was unloading another wooden bin from the flatbed truck at the opened garage door. As the forklift set down the apples by the tank, a little girl appeared, peering into the bin of discarded apples at the elbow of Lisa, a crew member. The little girl's copper-colored braids were a sure giveaway.

"Hey, there. Aren't you Piper's daughter?" Lance crouched down next to her. She whipped her head around, peering at him with all the trepidation those green eyes could hold. "You're fine. No need to be scared." He scanned the area for Piper, assuming she was somewhere close by. "Do you know your mom helped sort apples just like that?"

She picked at her lip, dipped her chin and glanced at Lisa from the corner of her eye.

"Here." Lance leaned over and grabbed an apple. "See that mark? That means this apple goes for pies and applesauce. So, we put it here." He set it down in the bin. "Just because it's marked up, doesn't mean it's no good. It's just got a different purpose than the pretty ones at the store."

Lance glanced around for Piper. Her daughter lifted her hand, set it on the edge of the sorter tray, then thrummed her fingers.

"Go ahead. You try." Lance remembered how quiet Piper was when they'd started their all-nighter. Seemed her daughter had the same trait.

The little girl picked up an apple, turned it around in her hand, then placed it in the bin.

Lance leaned over and checked it out. "Yep, that one was for pies. Good eye."

She flicked a gaze at him with a shadow of a smile.

"Is your mom around here?"

Her smile vanished, and she shook her head quickly.

"Oh, well, we should probably find her." Lance stood, found a freshly washed apple without a mark and handed it to her. "Here, um… Have a snack." He thought about Piper's advice her first day—snacks were always a success with kids.

The little girl took the apple, then frowned. "I can't eat this." Her voice was high-pitched, slightly raspy, and she spoke a muddled *s* sound.

"Why not?"

She tilted her chin up, gave an unamused smile and pointed to her missing front teeth. "See?" she lisped. "I can't bite very well right now."

Lance chuckled. "Ah, I guess slices might be easier."

"Yes, sir. Mom always puts peanut butter on them, too." Her little hand offered the apple back to him.

"That's okay. You can still keep it." Lance couldn't believe how this tiny girl encapsulated her mother so completely—freckles, hair, eyes. But not nearly as rambunctious as Piper-the-Great had been over the years. "Anyone ever tell you that you look like your mama?"

She nodded again while turning the apple around in her hand. "Mom says I am her mini-me, except my heart is bigger than hers. She says she learns lots from me."

"Your mom is a good person. So, you must be amazing."

The little girl's eyes gleamed, and she gave him a real smile. So bright. So authentically happy. "What's your name?"

"I am Lance. How about you?" He couldn't remember. He was horrible with names.

"I—I am Maelyn. And I am not really allowed to talk to strangers. But you know my mom, so I guess it's okay."

"I do. Let's go find her." He motioned with a wave of his arm, and instead of following behind him, Maelyn skipped next to him and grabbed his hand. Again, she looked up at him with a wide grin. Somehow, her little hand felt like a perfect fit in his. The residual gloom of the morning reminder about Tara seemed to disappear. All Lance could think about was protecting this little girl and finding her mom as soon as possible. Piper must be panicked.

They weaved in and out of customers and strollers and headed toward the tables with red-and-white umbrellas outside the café.

"Mom and Grandma were arguing right there." Maelyn pointed at an empty table. "I didn't want to listen to them fight, so I thought I would see where that man was going with all those apples."

Arguing? Lance could only imagine how upset Piper was this very minute. "I don't think you should have left without telling them. I am sure your mom is worried."

Maelyn didn't say anything, just kept her eyes on other little kids passing by. By the time they left the café area, she was pressed up against his side.

"Don't be scared, sweetheart. We'll find—"

"Maelyn!" Piper was over by the family's backyard fence. She was turned away from them, hurrying in the direction of the corn pool.

"Piper, over here!" Lance called out. "See, there's Mom." He pumped Maelyn's hand.

Instead of letting go, Maelyn squeezed his hand tighter. "Yay. Let's go tell her about the big bath for the apples."

Lance began to laugh but thought better of it when he noticed Piper's face.

She was as pale as the picket fence behind her, and instead of running up to her daughter, she was frozen, except for her quivering chin.

When Piper furiously prayed that Maelyn would show up that very second, all the panic coursing through her veins must have caused her distraught brain to dream up this unbelievable scenario.

Maelyn held fast to Lance's hand, and there was no bashful tint on her cheeks or fear in her eyes. In fact, her little girl clung close to the secure hand, nearly pressing her cheek affectionately against the masculine arm…of her daddy.

Piper blinked several times. Nope, not her imagination. This was happening.

As instantaneously as Piper's prayer was answered, her eyes blurred with long-suppressed tears. "Maelyn—" She stumbled forward, begging the moisture to absorb back into her frantic self so she wouldn't have to so obviously wipe away tears. "I've been looking all over for you." She blinked a few more times before daring to look up at Lance.

He gave an assured smile, reached out and squeezed her shoulder. "She's been safe and sound in the production area."

Piper matched his calm as best as she could.

"Mommy, he's not a stranger." She dropped Lance's hand then handed Piper an apple. "And he gave me this. Can you cut it up for me?"

"Sure, sweet girl." She took the apple, thankful for something to occupy her shaking hands. "Maelyn, you can't just wander off like that. You had Mommy and Grandma so scared."

Maelyn's shoulders sagged. "I know. Mr. Lance told me that, too."

Heat flooded Piper's face as she instinctually looked at Lance again.

He cleared his throat, then looked down at her daughter. "She's a good listener, I guess." His mouth tilted up in a half smile, and he patted Maelyn's head. "I don't think she'll walk away again."

"No, I won't." Maelyn shielded her mouth with a cupped hand, as if to hide what she was going to say from Lance. In a loud whisper, she said, "Just don't fight with Grandma." Her eyes pierced Piper as if she were also trying to impress her plea like a brand across Piper's forehead.

"Maelyn!" Piper's mom ran up to them and bundled Maelyn against her. "We were so worried. Where'd you run off to?"

"I'm safe." Maelyn's lisped words were muffled against Mom's blouse. "Mr. Lance took care of me."

"Thank you." Mom flashed a wide smile of appreciation.

"No problem." Lance turned to leave. "I'd never forget who she belonged to. Spitting image of you, Piper." He winked. Piper's face grew even hotter. "I'd better get back to it. Nice meeting you officially, Maelyn."

Maelyn lifted a hand with a sweet wave, like she used to when she was a toddler. Her beaming face was a sure sign—she was smitten with her father.

Piper knelt in front of Maelyn, who was leaning against her grandma's leg. "I am sorry we were arguing, Mae." She searched her daughter's eyes. Piper couldn't stand knowing that her conflict with Mom had pushed Maelyn away. What was her little girl thinking? The suffocating arguments with Garrett pressed in on Piper's memory… Little Maelyn hiding in her closet while Piper tried to keep her voice calm, begging Garrett to do the same. "Grandma and I will get it all figured out."

Maelyn furrowed her brow. "Maybe I could just come to work with you? I can help sort apples. Mr. Lance taught me how. Then Grandma can work as much as she wants."

Piper's heart sank. She had been worried about a man like Lance treating Maelyn indifferently, when she'd ignored her daughter to argue with Mom. A seven-year-old did not need to problem-solve her after-school care. But that was exactly what the adults in her life had put on the discussion table just a little bit ago. Mom needed to work an extra shift, and Piper's ease into the workforce was not cutting it. Piper needed a *real* job, as Mom had said. One that could cover daycare until Maelyn was old enough to stay home alone.

Mom squeezed Maelyn close. "Sweetie, you don't have to worry about that. Mommy and I will figure all that out. Don't you worry."

Piper surrendered a thank-you smile to Mom, one that also meant an apology for resisting the inevitable. Piper needed a more permanent job. But she suspected her return to the orchard wasn't about work at all. Lance's usual gentleness was ever present with her daughter, just like it had been with Piper these past couple weeks. What if her prayer to give Maelyn the best childhood had everything to do with knowing her daddy?

There was unfinished business that needed to be taken care of. And as much as Piper's stomach roiled with the trepidation of all that might happen, she knew it was time to tell Lance the truth about her daughter—his daughter.

# Chapter Twelve

The crew had proven themselves sufficient, so Lance headed to the café to grab some hot cider before heading to the pumpkin patch to pick up some show pieces for Sidney's decorations around the grounds.

As he waited for Marge to fill his order, Lance peered out the front door and spotted Piper in the parking lot, waving goodbye to her mom and Maelyn. Lance should have taken Maelyn to Piper right away instead of giving the little girl a lesson on apple-sorting. Piper had been frantic.

Maybe she could use a break between the fiasco and getting back to work.

"Hey, Marge. Can you make that two ciders?"

"Sure thing, boss," Marge chimed as she bustled along the counter with beverage dispensers and to-go cups. She filled the cups, secured them with lids and handed them to Lance.

"Thank you," he said and hurried toward the door, pushing it open with his hip while trying to keep the cider from spilling. Piper walked up the path toward him. When she saw him, she slowed—more like hesitated—like she wasn't sure if she should acknowledge him or not. Strange. She turned toward the metal building instead, lifting her hand in a weak wave.

"Hey, Piper. I got this for you."

"Oh, really?" She changed her course and walked over to him after all. "That was nice of you."

"I figured good ol' apple cider might help take away any lingering nerves."

Her freckles blended with the flush that appeared on her face.

"You know, after losing track of Maelyn."

A forced laugh burst from her lips. "Sure thing. That was scary."

"Do you want to head with me to the pumpkin patch before going back to the booth? I figured you might need a little breather."

Her face brightened. "Oh, um, sure. That would be nice." But as she turned to walk with him, he noticed her bite her lip and grimace.

They passed through the production area. Lance checked in with the crew then exited through the garage door to the truck. He opened the passenger door for Piper, and she hopped in, careful with her steaming cider.

As they turned onto the dirt lane, Lance placed his cider in the cupholder. "You know, even if Maelyn had gone to the other side of the orchard, she would have been safe. I wouldn't be so hard on yourself for losing track—"

"I know. I am okay." Piper took a sip of her cider. "If she was scared, she would have found an employee. And you found her first, so, it's all good."

Lance kept a snail's pace as they passed the attractions where groups of customers lingered. A couple little boys pointed at the truck and pumped their arms like they wanted him to honk the horn as if he were a semitruck driver.

"Those kids like the truck, I guess." He didn't want to scare everyone in the place with a honk, so Lance waved at the boys instead. They jumped up and down like he was a celebrity.

"Those boys might, but look at that little girl." Piper pointed to a curly-headed girl plugging her ears. "This diesel engine is loud. Maelyn wouldn't care for it, either. She's sensitive to noise."

"She seems like a sweet kid." He couldn't help but smile as he thought of Maelyn pointing out her missing teeth.

"She is." Piper's voice was quiet now. She ran her finger along the rim of her cup. Lance accelerated once all the customers were behind them. Piper shifted in her seat. "There's something I—I—" She glanced his way, then quickly turned to her window and lifted her cup to her lip. "I am worried about. Maelyn heard Mom and me discussing her childcare situation. Mom's going to take an extra shift, so I need to figure out after-school care."

"You know, Maelyn is welcome to come here after school. There's a bus stop just down by the Vander Walt farm."

Piper jerked around and faced him. "Really?"

Lance shrugged. "I don't see why it would be a huge problem. And besides, Maelyn has a great appreciation for the work we—*ahem*—I do." He slid a playful look at Piper and laughed. "I am sure she would be welcomed by the whole family. Just like another redhead I know." Wasn't that the truth? Piper was loved by every Hudson. His stomach flipped. And he shoved aside defining what love meant to each and every Hudson.

"Oh, wow, Lance. That would be amazing. I can't

believe how much she likes you. I guess being around Mom's husband has given her a second chance at trusting guys."

A sour wave crashed around in Lance's stomach. He thought about how timid Maelyn had been before warming up once Lance gave her some attention. "Garrett wasn't the nicest guy in high school, but surely having a daughter softened him."

Piper sputtered a cynical laugh. "Unfortunately, I swept all his flaws under the rug until it was too late."

"Why, Piper? Why'd you choose him? Do you realize how hurtful it was to see you go back to that guy? I mean, he didn't make great choices in high school. And you and I had grown close—"

"And you were moving across the country."

"Yeah, so?"

"Lance, we aren't going to hash all that—I mean, it is what it is now."

And she had a daughter from that choice. He sounded so petty bringing that up.

They didn't speak anymore. Lance had so many questions, but he couldn't get wrapped up in Piper Gray again. Yet he couldn't help but fume at the possibility of Garrett harming Maelyn in any way. The sweet girl had won Lance over in only a few minutes.

When they reached the pumpkin patch entrance, Piper seemed withdrawn once more, her weariness evident in the downward tug of her mouth. Lance hopped out of the truck and instinctually jogged around the cab to open Piper's door. She was already standing outside.

"Ever the gentleman," she jested, lowering in a clumsy curtsy. Her spark had returned, for a moment.

"I'm worried about you, Piper." Lance tried to look at Piper through the lens of a Hudson family member, although his heart was beating down his effort. He added, "And Maelyn."

She furrowed her forehead, a cavernous crease forming between her eyebrows.

"I just want to be sure you aren't in a bad situation—"

"I told you, that's behind me. He's not in our lives anymore."

"At all?" He rubbed the back of his neck, glancing around at the sprawling vines on either side of the truck. "I mean, your little girl is a sweetheart—" He gave an uneasy chuckle. He hadn't been around kids much. A few minutes with a wandering child didn't make him an expert.

"Lance. Garrett wants nothing to do with us. And it's mutual—for both Maelyn and me." Her jaw was flinching as if she were grinding her teeth. Maybe she was. There was no snark in her eyes, nor weariness. They were vibrant with determination.

"I'm sorry. I guess I just don't get how a dad can be so distant from his kid… I mean, I would never…" Ugh. He grimaced and looked away on a deep inhale. Old disappointment was clutching at his throat. He had planned so much that had dissolved so quickly. His longing for a family was not easily erased by this change of scenery, no matter his marital status.

"Lance?" Piper was closer to him now. She spoke as if she had said his name more than once. Her emotional glimmer had melted into a genuine concern.

Lance realized he was glowering. "I never realized how much I wanted kids, until Tara decided she didn't want to have kids with me. We started going through the process of fertility treatments…" And he had mentioned returning to Iowa to raise their family. "I guess all my enthusiasm for a family scared her straight into someone else's arms."

"Oh, I am so sorry, Lance." Piper reached out and placed her hand on his forearm. "But wanting a family is a really good thing." Her voice shrank with each word. "I—I can't imagine having someone who wanted kids as much as me."

"Me neither, I guess. We'd talked about it, and she'd gone in for the initial appointment. But it was all for show. At first, she thought having kids would make our marriage better, so she said. But then I was planning out a future she wanted nothing to do with. That's when she admitted to having an affair."

Piper's eyes bubbled with moisture as she slid her hand down his arm to his fingers. She clutched them tight. "Lance, I need to tell you something. Maybe we should sit down." She nodded to the new benches Sidney had installed along the main pathway.

"I shouldn't have said anything. Don't worry about me." Embarrassment flooded his chest but he didn't want to let go of her hand just yet. Piper was grounding him to this brighter future beyond his valley walking. His college freshman self should have never let her go. Why had he not put up a fight?

"Come on." Piper tugged his hand and led him to the bench. She withdrew her fingers and folded her hands in her lap, her jaw still working.

Lance lowered next to her. They faced most of his family's land. The green canopies of apple trees sprung up between the sprawling pumpkin vines and the distant rooftops of the Hudson house, the metal building, the corn pool shed and the small café. Hudson Orchard was home.

He couldn't focus on what might have been. There

was no such thing. Lance Hudson was not a great predictor of the future. Who'd have thought he would sit here now, with Piper, and none of his might-haves had ever…been?

Since the moment Lance had handed her a cup of cider, Piper had had a debate squawking inside her mind—*tell him… No, not yet!* But now, after Lance had poured his heart out about wanting kids of his own, the thought of keeping this secret to herself was unbearable. The only thing she had to lose was her friendship with the Hudsons. That would be heart-wrenching—for Piper. But this really wasn't about Piper. She'd made it about herself far too long. This was affecting the lives of people she truly cared about. Piper had no doubt in her mind that Lance would be a stable father figure to Maelyn. Lance Hudson would become the father— had been all along—that any little girl would dream of having. Piper had never met her own father, who'd passed away in active duty when she was a baby. But she would be overjoyed for her little girl to have a dad who loved her.

How could she keep his daughter a secret any longer?

"Lance, Garrett was never a dad to Maelyn. He was so caught up in partying, he didn't really have time for us. I mean, at first, he was super attentive to me. But then he got into some pretty bad things. I didn't really know the extent of it until last year." She closed her eyes and shook her head, as if trying to get rid of memories. "Until Maelyn… Maelyn found drugs in his drawer."

"What did you do?"

"Well, it was the first time I had leverage. I told Garrett to seek help or we would leave. Once he refused, I threatened to get the authorities involved. He pretty much opened the door for us to go." She shook her head. "For years, Garrett kept a tight hold on our money, the car, the phone—everything that gave me a chance to connect to the outside world was attainable only if Garrett said so. I didn't realize how stuck I was until we had to miss some of Maelyn's well-check appointments. And by that point, it was just so hard to not believe the criticisms Garrett would say to me. First, I was neglecting him for the baby. Then, I messed up dinner or didn't tidy up just right. He'd leave for days, and we would struggle..." Her voice surrendered to a sneer. "I finally realized what lured him away."

"Sounds like he gave up so much for an addiction." Lance threaded his fingers through hers again.

Tears pricked the back of her eyes.

"That's the thing. No matter if he tried to play the role of being Maelyn's dad, he knew he wasn't." She breathed in a jagged breath. Lance's expression didn't change. He didn't understand what she was saying. "And knowing the truth made letting go easy for him."

"The truth?" Lance cocked his head.

"The truth is, Lance—" Piper squeezed his hand tight. He placed his other hand over both of their hands. A sign of security—something Piper had longed for and never really received. "The truth is, Garrett isn't Maelyn's father." She squeezed his hand again, and said, "You are."

# Chapter Thirteen

Those pumpkin vines may as well have wound their way up Lance's shaking leg, wrapped around his torso and squeezed out all his breath. He couldn't move. He couldn't see anything but Piper's lips moving as she called his name and searched his face for a response.

"Lance?"

He let go of her hands and rose to his feet. "You can't be serious?"

Piper rose and reached a hand to him. "Lance, let me explain."

He stepped back, glaring at her. "You'd better."

"I—I found out the week before you left for Stanford. I had been miserable knowing you were leaving but you had worked so hard for that scholarship. And then the positive test could have ruined it. Garrett showed up after being gone all summer and wanted to make up. I just thought it was perfect timing. He seemed a better match for me anyway."

"So, you had *my* baby without telling me?" Lance's voice was scratchy and strained. "That's not right. You don't get to choose those things, Piper."

"I was eighteen and scared. When Garrett tried to make amends, I figured that was the best plan. I didn't deserve a guy like you—and I sure wasn't going to mess up the hopes your whole family had for the first Hudson to go to college."

"You didn't deserve a guy like me? But you were pregnant...with...with..." Lance ran his hands through his hair, the emotion gripping his throat like a vice. He had a daughter? "With my little girl?" Tears stung his eyes. He squeezed them tight, swiveling away from her.

He had a daughter.

Maelyn Gray was his daughter.

He was a daddy.

Piper was next to him. "I am so sorry, Lance." Her cell phone rang. She answered, "Hey, Sid. Not a great time... Oh. We'll be right up." She ended the call. "Maelyn and Mom are at the orchard booth with Sid. Mom's cell doesn't have any service out here. They are looking for Maelyn's locket. She's...she's pretty upset." Piper's voice was shaky. She fiddled with her own necklace.

Lance began to walk to the truck, his heart pounding at the thought of seeing the little girl again, as a father. They both climbed in the truck. Piper turned to speak, but Lance just couldn't listen to one more excuse.

He lifted his hand and muttered, "Please, no more talking."

Only the diesel engine roared in the silence while Lance recalled the short romance between himself and the mother of his child. What could all this mean for him? Why would he miss out on so much of his daughter's life? Seven years. A lot of living happened in those years. *What might have been* had already happened. He balled his fist against the steering wheel as they stopped at the orchard booth.

Piper hopped out of the truck and ran up, scooping Maelyn into a big hug. Lance strode over.

His little girl had tears streaming down her cheeks. "We'll never find it, Mama. I lost it forever!"

"We can look. I will leave no apple unplucked if that's what it takes." Piper kissed Maelyn's nose.

Sidney finished up with a customer and leaned on the counter. "Okay, Miss Maelyn. We've got our reinforcements. Your mom can take you to the tree you harvested, and Lance can take Grandma down to the café area. Oh, and the corn pool—" Sidney's eyes grew big like the fruit piled up next to her. She exchanged a skeptical glance with Lance. Finding a necklace in the corn pool would be near impossible.

"Mr. Lance, do you think it fell in the tank?" Maelyn sniffled and rubbed her nose with her knuckle.

Lance tried to activate the voice that was struggling to work in this moment. "I've got a better idea. Can I take Maelyn to look for it? We'll find that necklace." He held out his hand, ignoring all the women staring at him. He steadied his eyes on his daughter. Lance had missed out on enough time with his child.

Piper followed behind Maelyn, who was clutching Lance's hand. "I can go with you all."

"Do you mind if we go alone?" Lance asked. "I'd love some time. Won't say a thing."

Piper cinched her brows together then inhaled and exhaled visibly. "Sure. Let me know if you find it."

"Will do." He walked with Maelyn to the truck and opened the passenger door for her.

The least that woman could do was give him a chance to help his daughter.

* * *

The last time Piper thought the world was caving in was the day she'd left Garrett without a penny to her name. She had stood on the street, with Maelyn clinging to her leg, and wondered how they would manage to get from Waterloo to Rapid Falls. Her neighbor allowed Piper to use her phone to call Mom. About thirty minutes later, a friend of Bill's picked them up in a similar truck to the one that now drove away with her little girl sitting next to a man she really didn't know. But that man knew something Maelyn did not. Piper hoped he would keep his word about not saying anything to Maelyn.

"You okay, Piper?" Sidney approached. "You look queasy."

"Um… I just…" She bounced her gaze from her best friend to the taillights of the truck that was disappearing down the hill. "I… I have royally messed up, Sidney."

"What happened? Lance seemed off."

Piper walked over to the booth with her arms crossed over her chest. As soon as she'd spilled the truth to Lance, regret had overwhelmed her—not because she'd told him, but because she hadn't. How could she withhold that father–daughter relationship from a guy like Lance? From any Hudson? Now, she faced her best friend, who'd unconditionally welcomed Piper back into life at Hudson Orchard.

Mom was waiting by the gate. "Are you coming, Piper?"

"Just a minute. Mom, you'll want to hear what I have to say." May as well just lay it all out so she could release herself from the secret once and for all. She turned and leaned against the counter.

Mom stood to the left of Piper, and Sidney stood on

her right. She didn't know who to look at, so she just stared down at her sneakers. Scuffed at the toes. Loosely tied. Slightly too tight, but all she had. And they didn't matter at all. What mattered most to Piper was her little girl. And now was the time to own the scuffs and much-too-tight grip she had on protecting her.

"Today, I told Lance—" She boomeranged a glance from one woman to the other. Both gave her their full attention. "I told Lance the truth. Maelyn is his daughter."

"What?" Sidney screeched. She pushed away from the counter.

"Oh, Piper. Is that really true?" Mom whispered. Piper felt the sting of judgment in her words, but Mom's face was filled with compassion.

Piper slowly turned to face Sidney. "Sidney, it all happened so quickly, and I just wasn't thinking back then… I was so immature and full of myself…and—"

Sidney threw her arms around Piper and hugged her tight. "Lance must be over the moon."

What? She was happy about all this? "No, no. He's not. He's pretty much devastated."

Sidney pulled away. "Well, sure. The initial shock. But do you know how long Lance has wanted kids?" Her blue eyes filled with tears. "After all that's gone wrong for him, this is finally something right."

Piper shook her head. "I am glad you see it that way. But he's really upset with me. He doesn't understand how I could cut him out of the equation."

Sidney swiped at her eyes. "How could you?" Her question wasn't interrogatory but seeking a matter-of-fact answer.

Piper glimpsed her mom's chest move with a big intake of air from the corners of her eyes. Piper couldn't answer fully. Not with Mom there. Piper had never considered that, while she was so worried about the Hudsons passing judgment on her, she had held them on a pedestal all her life. They were the perfect family, and hers had hardly been one at all. Piper was the mistake-maker, a trait her mom seemed to have over the years, too. A niggle tugged at her conscience. Had Piper protected Lance out of some weird inferiority complex?

Sidney shifted as she waited for Piper to answer. Mom did the same.

"Garrett seemed a better match for me." He had been going straight to work as a mechanic. Heading to Waterloo to get away from his own dysfunctional family in Rapid Falls. "Lance had big plans ahead. And Garrett wanted to get back together. It was an easy fix." She rolled her eyes. "That turned out to be my biggest mistake ever."

Lance's palms were slightly sweating as they traveled down the road. Maelyn was no longer crying but pressing her nose against the window of the passenger door. They quickly caught up with the hayride on the road ahead. Lance slowed his speed to follow safely behind it.

"Maelyn, you all went on the hayride, right?"

"Uh-huh."

"We'll look there first. I'll introduce you to one of my favorite people." Lance noticed his dad on the tractor, the slight slope of his shoulders and the salt-and-pepper hair beneath the Hudson orchard hat. Lance slid his gaze to Maelyn, the newest Hudson grand-daughter.

While he had often thought about that summer with Piper, he had tried to ignore the fact they had taken things too far that first weekend. But what followed had been a sweet secret romance of stealing kisses and holding hands when nobody was around. When August hit, he had wanted to suggest a long-distance relationship—but then he found out Piper went back to Garrett. Lance cared more than she had, it seemed. Lance ground his teeth. How could she have chosen that Garrett guy over him? They could have made it work.

He would have done anything to be with his child… with Piper.

No, he couldn't go there. His jaw ached with the tension of all he considered. What Piper had done by keeping him oblivious to this little girl next to him was unacceptable. She'd even worked at the orchard for several days without one word. He looked at Maelyn once more. Her broad forehead and little curls along her hairline were clearly Hudson.

Maelyn caught his gaze. She pointed as she spoke, "Is that man on the tractor your favorite person?"

"Huh? Oh, yes." *Grandpa, to you.* When would Maelyn find out? He wouldn't tell her without Piper. Including Piper on anything to do with Maelyn was the right thing to do. Even if Piper hadn't given him the same courtesy. "That's my dad. Mr. Hudson."

"Hudson! Mommy always talks about the Hudsons. She tells me to be a good friend like a Hudson." Maelyn kicked her heel against the seat. "It's like you are famous." She flashed a broad toothless smile at him. His heart melted more than he'd ever thought it could.

"I don't know about famous. But Rapid Falls likes us." *And soon, you'll be able to join in the fame, sweetheart.* If only Lance could cool his anger toward Piper, and if only he could avoid being asked about an attraction he'd tried so hard to forget. Sidney knew, but his parents would have plenty of questions. All they thought was that Piper was an annoying-to-Lance welcomed-surrogate member of the family, not his first love.

The hayride slowed to a stop at the station, and Lance parked the truck. "Come on, sweetheart. Let's go look around. Think you remember where you sat?"

Maelyn nodded, scooted along the bench seat, then held her hand out to him. He gently held onto her as she stepped down onto the running board, then jumped into the grass. Seven years, and yet, she was still so little.

"C'mon, Mr. Lance. That necklace is very special." Her lisp made her seem little, too. Lance smiled and followed her to the hayride.

After the last person unloaded, Maelyn let go of his hand and ran up the steps. "We sat over here." She went to a hay bale in the far corner.

Dad walked over. "Who's that little girl?"

"Uh, that's Piper's daughter." Lance swallowed hard.

Dad chuckled. "Can't believe I asked. Yep, that's Piper right there."

Maelyn skulked over. "It's not there."

"Really?" Lance climbed the steps and stood next to her. He put a hand on her shoulder. "Why don't I take a look to be sure? Okay?"

With her chin lowered, Maelyn nodded.

"What are you looking for?" Dad asked.

Maelyn's head jerked up, and she drew close to Lance, reaching for his hand again. "It's okay, Maelyn," Lance said. "This is my dad. We talked about him in the truck."

Dad narrowed his eyes at Lance while grinning wide.

Maelyn leaned into Lance's thigh and cupped her hand over her mouth, then whispered, "He's a Hudson, right?"

"Yes," Lance whispered back, his grin as wide as his dad's.

Maelyn dropped her hand and then said, "I lost my necklace, Mr. Hudson." Her little lip wobbled. Lance squeezed her hand. Really, he wanted to scoop her up like he'd seen Piper do, give her a giant hug and take away any pain.

Wow, this fatherhood instinct had come on fast.

Dad propped his foot on the bottom step and leaned his elbow on his knee. "Just a minute, Maelyn." He dug in his shirt pocket and pulled out a necklace. "Is this what you're looking for?" A silver chain swung from his finger, and a heart shaped locket glinted in the late-afternoon sun.

Maelyn gasped and ran down the steps. "That's it, Mr. Hudson. Where'd you find it?" She reached out and took the necklace carefully.

"Well, someone found it and turned it in. There are some pretty great people in these parts, I'd say." He winked at Maelyn, then stood up straight. "And one of those people is Marge. I'm hoping she's got some hot cider left. And maybe a snickerdoodle or two. Maelyn, have you had any hot cider today?"

She pressed her locket to her heart and shook her head. "No, sir."

"Well, that is something that is a must at Hudson Orchard. Lance, you should take this young lady straight to the café."

"Can you put my necklace on first?" Maelyn turned to Lance and handed him the locket.

"Sure thing." He admired the simple silver heart. "What's inside?"

"A prayer. Mama gave it to me on my first day of school." She pulled her braids in front of her shoulders. "She's got the same one."

Lance unclasped the necklace, tempted to open the

heart but not quite feeling he had permission to do so. And he wasn't going to ask. He placed the necklace over her head and hooked the clasp. "There. It's very secure. Shouldn't come off again."

"Unless I take it off." Maelyn spun around and grinned wide at her own wit.

"Right." Lance squeezed her shoulder.

Dad's gaze glimmered Lance's way. He adjusted his hat and said, "Will you all join me for some cider, or is Piper waiting?"

"You know my mom, too?" Maelyn said to Dad, hopping down the steps. "Maybe she's famous just like you."

Dad chuckled and held out his hand to the little girl. She hesitated, then slowly lifted her hand to his and began to walk with him. Lance followed close behind and texted Piper the news about the necklace and where they would be. He then tried to calm all the emotions that warred inside him—regret, anger and an almost instantaneous love for his daughter.

## Chapter Fourteen

**W**hen Piper got Lance's text, she and Mom began to walk along the path toward the main area.

"I didn't even know you and Lance dated," Mom said, slightly out of breath as she lagged behind.

Piper realized she was in hyper-speed. She slowed for Mom to catch up, even though she'd rather just run and avoid any discussion. "We'd kept it a secret, and it was only for the summer. I was at the Hudsons' all the time, and Sidney was working at a camp. Better than—" Piper bit her lip. She gave Mom a sideways glance.

Mom fluttered her lashes and waved her hand. "Don't hush for me. I was there. We both dealt with your former stepdad in different ways. I was always so thankful you had the Hudsons for a soft place to land." She stopped and placed a hand on Piper's arm. "One of my greatest regrets is pushing you away." Fine lines fanned out from her sage-colored eyes as she searched Piper's.

"I really wasn't sure you'd noticed."

"It was hard to know how to be a wife to that man and a mother to you."

"Life doesn't wait for you to be ready, huh?" Piper repeated Mom's sentiment from earlier when they'd discussed single parenting. She now understood Mom a little better.

"I am so sorry, Piper. I should have been there for you." A barrier crumbled away between Piper and her mom.

"Thanks, Mom. I am so glad for second chances. And Bill is amazing."

While Mom had managed what life threw at her one way, Piper had gone her own way for eight years. Both Gray women finally took steps in the better direction, even if it had taken a while. They threaded their arms together, and they continued to walk.

When they reached the main area, she saw Lance, Don and Maelyn sitting on the café patio. "There she is," Piper managed to say around the instant lump in her throat.

They walked up to the group. Maelyn was swinging her legs and sipping from a to-go cup. Lance saw Piper first. His mouth flattened to a thin slit, and he glowered at his own cup.

"Hey, there." Piper's high pitch sounded far away.

Maelyn lifted her cup. "I have hot cider, Mommy. But Miss Marge put some ice cubes in it so it won't burn my tongue."

"Well, that's thoughtful of her." Mom smiled and greeted Don.

Piper crouched down next to Maelyn, turning her back to the obviously fuming new father. "Where'd you find your necklace?"

"On the hayride." Maelyn pulled out her locket from under her T-shirt. "Mr. Hudson found it, actually."

"A customer is to thank for that." Don stood. "I'd better get back and make the last round. It was very nice meeting you, Maelyn." He held out his hand. Maelyn scrunched her nose and just stared.

"Go on, honey," Mom coached. "Just give him a shake. It's a very grown-up thing to do."

Maelyn shook his hand.

"Nice firm grip. That's good." Don winked. He patted Lance's shoulder and said, "See you later, son," then walked around the table. As he passed Piper, Don murmured, "Sweet kid you have there, Piper. I wouldn't expect anything less, having a mom like you." He gave her a playful punch to the arm and continued on his way.

Lance sprang from his seat and stood within inches of Piper. His glower was full-on, but true hurt tipped his eyebrows upward. "Can we talk?"

"Yeah, sure. Mae, Mom—we'll be right back." Piper shoveled in breath and led the way to a quiet spot near the parked utility vehicle, her Lance-drawn carriage from days ago. Whoa, this was no time for jokes. Lance stood facing her now, his arms tight across his chest, the veins bulging in his forearms and his face red with emotion.

Lance couldn't help but notice that Piper was obviously nervous. She dropped her attention to the banged-up utility vehicle, tracing the dents with her finger. Her profile was the same as their daughter's. *Their* daughter's. If he had been standing across from this woman a few years ago, knowing that they would have a child together, he doubted anger would have played any part in his reaction. But now, she'd crossed so many lines, he wondered if they were still in Falls County.

"Piper. I want Maelyn to know who I am."

"I know, I know." She only nodded but didn't look at him.

"Today. Now."

She fluttered her lashes as she turned to face him.

She took a short intake of air, then caught his gaze with her green gems. "Lance, I know you are anxious to let her know. But I need to prepare what I am going to say…"

"Does she think Garrett is her dad?"

She shook her head, the little crevice between her brows deepened. "Couldn't let her ever think that."

"Then who did you say her dad was?"

Piper lifted her shoulders and slapped her hands to her side. "I just tell her she's a blessing. And that her daddy thought she was pretty special, but he couldn't be with us now."

Lance's nostrils flared as he considered all the instances his daughter had probably asked about him and received that answer. It wasn't a bad explanation, but it fell short of painting him the kind of father he wanted to be. "I would have always been there for her if I'd known."

Piper dropped her gaze again.

Lance drew closer to her, remembering that this woman had been through a tough time, regardless of this giant secret. He didn't want to hurt her more than she'd already been hurt. Even after what she'd done. He hooked his finger under her chin. Her eyes rounded. "Piper Gray, you've made me so mad today. And I don't think that's going to go away any time soon." His vision blurred. Ah, his emotions were out of control. "But please, let Maelyn know I am her dad."

Piper reached up and wiped a tear sliding down his cheek, then cupped his jaw with her hand. "Okay, Lance. We'll tell her. Together."

*Thank you* was on the tip of his tongue. But like he'd admitted, he was still mad. Sad. Overjoyed. Overwhelmed. All the emotions that were way beyond the gamut of emotions he thought he'd run this past year.

Piper slid her hand away and walked ahead of him. Quickly, he swiped his eyes with the back of his hand and followed her to Maelyn and Karen.

"I spy… Mommy!" Maelyn giggled.

"And Lance Hudson." Karen gave a quick nod to Lance. He tipped his baseball cap, but his chest was tight with nerves.

Piper sat next to Maelyn, and Lance sat across from her. "Hey, Mae. I want to tell you something really important."

"Can we get some more snickerdoodles first?"

"How about I go grab those?" Mom rose, dipping her head at Piper in a knowing nod of approval. "Be right back." She patted Lance's hand on her way to the café entrance.

Lance's spine stiffened, realizing that this was probably the most important day of his life.

Piper reached over and held Maelyn's hand. "Remember when I said your daddy can't be with us?"

Maelyn's amusement faded, and she nodded quickly, then started fiddling with her lip.

"Hey, sweet girl. It's okay." Piper stood and gathered the little girl onto her lap. "I have some really good news." She gave Maelyn a giant kiss on her neck.

Maelyn squealed, then watched Piper's mouth out of the corners of her eyes as Piper said, "Lance is your daddy, Maelyn. I just didn't know how to tell you." Now it was Piper's turn to shed a tear. She pressed her cheek to Maelyn's.

Lance suddenly felt awkward. Should he be here? Maelyn didn't look at him right away. She only pressed her hand to her mom's cheek and patted it gently.

But all of a sudden, the little girl's gaze shifted to Lance. Her cheek parted from Piper's. Maelyn said in a raspy voice, "You're my...daddy?" Her brow was muddled with confusion. She surveyed his face. "Mr. Lance is my daddy?" She jerked her head back and looked at Piper.

Piper only nodded.

Maelyn craned her neck toward Lance and lifted her hands up in question. "What took you so long to find us?"

Lance reached over and squeezed her knee. "I'm here now, sweetheart." Maelyn pushed her head away and rested against her mom's shoulder, but tears began to streak her face. Lance wiped her cheeks with his thumbs. "I'm so glad you came to the orchard today."

"Me, too." She cocked her head, wiped her nose with the back of her hand and gave him a large, toothless smile. Piper kissed Maelyn's temple and visibly sighed. Again, Lance wanted to thank Piper, but something was eating away at him that tarnished her golden smile and dimmed her sparkling eyes. His daughter would always think that somehow, Lance had chosen to stay away all these years. Somehow, Lance had thought she should be with that guy Garrett instead of him.

Piper had tried to protect her little girl with an excuse for Lance's absence. But only Lance would reap those consequences.

And because of that, he just wouldn't be able to look at Piper the same, ever again.

# Chapter Fifteen

Piper trailed behind as Lance, Mom and Maelyn headed to Mom's car. All Piper could think about was how Lance's expression back at the café table reminded her of the days when he would act annoyed with Piper after one of her and Sidney's escapades...before they leaned into each other that summer.

Today, Piper had seen the irritation again. She and Lance may have survived similar heartaches of divorce and rejection, but his strong and steady trait was still obvious. He demanded to place everything out in the open, while Piper's confidence had shrunk to the size of an apple seed.

Mom opened the back door to her sedan.

Maelyn hopped in. "See you soon!" She waved to Lance but flashed a worried look at Piper.

"Once that bus route gets figured out, you'll get to spend time at the orchard." Lance leaned his hand on the car and craned his neck to smile at Maelyn. "You can help me get the pumpkin patch ready." He shifted his eyes to Piper in a sideways kind of way. "That is... if your mama is okay with that."

She shrugged her shoulders. "Whatever Maelyn

wants." Yes, this was all about Maelyn. Every step away from Garrett's duplex to this very moment.

"Can we make a pumpkin carriage like in Cinderella?" Maelyn clasped her hands together.

Lance chuckled. "Not sure we have a big enough pumpkin, or a fairy godmother around here. But you can help set up the display at the entrance."

"Okay!" Maelyn was truly delighted in every way. But as Lance stepped away, Piper noticed familiar anxiety in her daughter's eyes.

Mom got in the driver's seat and closed her door. Piper approached Maelyn while Lance began to walk away backward, sticking his hands in his pockets.

"See you later, Maelyn." Lance winked, tipped his hat, then spun on his heel without any acknowledgment of Piper.

Piper bent down and leaned into the car, giving Maelyn a kiss on the cheek.

Instantly, Maelyn grabbed her neck and smashed Piper's face against her braids. "Mom, I don't want to live here."

Piper yanked her head away. "What?"

Maelyn's green eyes swam in tears. "I—I like Mr. Lance. But…can I still live with you?"

"Oh, sweet girl." Piper wrapped her arms so tight around her little girl, she was afraid she might steal her breath away. Easing up, she faced her again. "You will always live with me. Don't you ever worry about that."

Maelyn nodded and exhaled dramatically. "Good."

"I am going to make sure everything is finished up with Auntie Sid, then I will be home soon, okay?" Maelyn nodded and kicked her legs on the seat.

"Ice cream?" Piper tilted her head and hooked an investigative eyebrow.

"Yes!" Maelyn lisped as sweet as could be, and Piper closed the door.

She surrendered a tight smile to Mom, who did the same, then Piper stepped away from the vehicle.

As she crossed the parking lot, her confidence suddenly sprouted. Anger coursed through her as she considered exactly what the strong and steady Lance had just forced upon them. He'd hardly given Piper the chance to consider how and when to tell Maelyn about him. How had Piper allowed another person to control the situation? To control her?

Lance was heading to the house, taking the porch steps slowly.

Piper jogged down the sidewalk and planted herself at the bottom of the steps just as Lance reached for the front door. "Hey." She placed her hands on her sides, more because she was out of breath and had a slight cramp, but the strong stance was a good cover to hide any cowardice that tried to dissuade her.

Lance turned. "Piper. What's up?" As if nothing ginormous had just happened! But as he approached the top step, she noticed the hollow stare set directly through her.

Piper swallowed hard, wondering if her voice might come out screechy, or if she was as empowered as she'd been seconds ago. "Look," she said in a rather cool tone. "I know it wasn't right for me to keep Maelyn from you, but—" Her throat tightened. The next words came out with threadbare strength. "Do you realize the frailty of this situation…for Maelyn? I am her only security right now."

Lance scowled at her as he loped down the steps and stood across from her. "How is knowing her father not secure?"

"That's not what I meant." Piper stepped back even though they were a good five or six feet apart. "I mean that it would have been nice for you and me to discuss how to tell her exactly. Maybe even wait until she got to know you better."

"Like she got to know you for the last seven years?" He huffed, drawing his eyebrows into a zigzag of sarcasm.

"You know what I mean. She is nervous. She was worried that she wouldn't live with me anymore." Piper lowered her gaze, trying to curb her emotion. "You've given her a good first impression, but these things take time."

Lance hooked his hand on his neck and glared into the distance just past Piper. "Didn't have to," he mumbled.

Piper glanced about the white siding of the house and the shaded wraparound porch. This place was a mansion in her childhood mind. So much of her existence as a child felt like she was the pauper girl taken under the wing of the generous family who lived life propped on this hill of comfort and loyalty.

"I had much more at stake than you."

"Oh, really?"

"Yes, Lance. Back then, the thought of upsetting your family with an unplanned pregnancy was as scary as raising a baby all by my lonesome." *And when the likes of me disrupts the ambitions of a golden boy...* "Maybe I made the wrong choice. But right now, for the sake of my daughter—"

Lance grimaced.

"—*our* daughter, we need to make future decisions carefully."

Any tightness fell away from his face, and he em-

braced Piper with rounded blue eyes only. She saw his
own vulnerability in their exchange. Like a little boy
wondering if he'd be reprimanded or accepted. "Piper,
you rejected me. You went back to…him…and I was
in love with you."

"What? I didn't think you took me seriously."

"After the time we spent together, that was your take-
away?" He shook his head then steadied his gaze on
her. "It doesn't matter now. Like you said, for the sake
of our daughter. I just want to be included."

Piper took a step closer. "Lance, I will include you. I
just need you to give me a chance to think first."

He gave a curt nod, then breathed in a deep, stuttered breath. Only a clapping cottonwood and the distant chatter from the café area filled her head. Or at
least, pressed in upon the echoing admission from
Lance Hudson. *I was in love with you.* Lance turned
toward the stairs, his head lowered.

"Okay. Well, I am going to see if Sidney needs any
help. I've pretty much blown my hours today." Piper
felt the shadow of a chuckle gather in the back of her
throat, but she was emotionally exhausted.

Lance paused and turned around again. "Does Sid
know?"

Piper nodded. "I just told her when you took Maelyn
to look for her necklace."

He furrowed his brow and stared at the house. "Piper,
should we tell my parents…together?"

"Sure. Okay." He didn't move. "Um, now?"

"As good a time as any."

"True." As Piper followed Lance up the stairs, she
felt as though she was shrinking—maybe sinking. This
fresh start had led her straight to exposing roots that
hadn't been hers to bury in the first place.

\* \* \*

Lance held open the door to Piper, and they both walked into the small foyer. The sound of Amelia's babble and Mom's baby talk carried from the four seasons room. Dad looked their way from the kitchen.

"Hey, you two."

"Hey, Dad," Lance rasped. He cleared his throat and led the way to the kitchen. The weight of everything that had happened pressed down on him. He took in a giant breath and braced himself with a hand splayed on the countertop. He couldn't believe it. So much longing to start a family, and he had had a daughter all along.

Piper sat on a barstool, her face a shade paler than usual, and she was fiddling with her prayer locket.

He recalled her talking about God having a lot to do with bringing her back to Rapid Falls. Lance couldn't get on board with such assumptions.

He'd come back to expand the family business. To escape a daily encounter with the ex-wife who'd broken his heart into a million pieces. A creeping hunch traveled its way up his spine.

To get to know a daughter he never knew about?

The coordination of two lives crashing into one seemed pretty unbelievable. But when Lance had woken up this morning, having a kid seemed unbelievable, too.

"Hey, there, kids." Mom breezed past him with Amelia on her hip. "Thought I heard the front door."

"Piper and I want to talk with you all." Lance wondered what this might have been like as a teen. Much more difficult. A wave of compassion filled his chest as he crossed over to Piper. Mom and Dad were never intimidating folks. But to an unwed pregnant teen? "The summer before I left for Stanford, Piper and I spent a lot of time together, and we didn't tell anyone, but we were kind of dating—"

Piper stood up. "I made a huge mistake, Don and Janet." Her lip was wobbling and her neck flushed with red streaks. "And trust me, I've paid big-time for that mistake." She turned to Lance with a wild surrender in her eyes. "You went to college, started a career and have grown into this great person, Lance. I couldn't hold you back." Tears began to bubble in her eyes. "Don't you see? We probably would have been those bitter people arguing over custody at this point if I hadn't—"

"Custody?" Mom tossed a confused look to Dad.

Lance placed a hand on Piper's shoulder. She was shaking. "What we want to tell you is that Maelyn is my daughter." He boomeranged a look between his parents. They both seemed frozen, just staring. Piper sank back into her stool. The words coming from his lips invigorated him and terrified him. Piper had said that Maelyn was nervous. She was the one girl he never wanted to overwhelm or push away. How could Lance be the father she needed when the little girl had seven years to wonder why he'd never shown up?

"We have another granddaughter?" Mom held Amelia close, her cheek on the baby's soft dark hair.

"She's a sweet one," Dad added. "Lance, you just found out?"

"Yes, just today."

Mom and Dad exchanged glances, then focused on each of them with stoic expressions. Mom said in a soft voice, "Piper, you should have come to us. We've always taken care of you when you were in trouble." She rounded the kitchen island toward Piper. "But this…this would have been us caring for both of you."

Piper only nodded. His parents began to discuss when

they might be able to get to know Maelyn, and Piper shared that she would be changing bus routes. Lance felt as though they were in this weird bubble, planning for his long-lost dream to become a reality. About seven years overgrown.

## Chapter Sixteen

The next morning, Piper walked into the metal building with anticipation greater than her first day on the job. She was the mother of a sweet little Hudson and the woman Lance Hudson once loved. Would knowing Lance cared so deeply for her back then have convinced her to reject Garrett and follow her own heart?

As she clocked in, Lance offered her a smile, curt and restrained, jolting Piper from what might have been to what was now. A twinge of regret pinched her conscience. Don and Sidney were discussing the upcoming Rapid Falls Harvest Festival, and as Sidney's voice piqued with excitement, Lance's brows went up with his usual smirk.

"So, should we offer something at the end of the parade? Maybe free apple cider?" Sidney wondered. "Any ideas, you two?"

Piper tried to tame her fluttering stomach at Sid's grouping her with Lance. How silly—how high school. But she did have an idea. "You know, if it's the same route as before, you'll end pretty close to the women's shelter. They are always looking for fresh produce."

"Oh, really?" Sidney placed her coffee mug on the counter. "We have that, for sure."

"How much are you thinking?" Lance chimed in.

"I don't know. They house ten mothers at a time." Piper walked over to the discard bin. "I was thinking about it while we sorted. There are some perfectly fine apples that only have a mark or two. I would have been so thankful to have some when I was—" The flutters from before turned to lead wings. She shot a look to each Hudson, not wanting to share about her own stay at the shelter when she'd tried to get away from Garrett. Mom hadn't been home, and she'd been too embarrassed to stay with the Hudsons after three years of hiding Maelyn's paternity. "I mean, when you are tight on money, fresh produce is amazing."

"I am sure we can add some cream-of-the-crop apples, too?" Don questioned Lance.

"Probably. Good idea, Piper." Lance took a sip from his travel mug, and weirdly, Piper warmed as if she'd drunk hot coffee herself.

Her cell vibrated. It was the school. She stepped away while the Hudsons discussed the festival further. Piper talked with the transportation director. Seemed that Maelyn could switch as early as today. She would contact the school secretary to pass the change on to Mae.

When Piper got off the phone, she told everyone the plan. Maelyn was heading here this afternoon. Piper would be finishing up with the final customers, so Lance offered to meet her at the stop.

"Promise to bring her straight to see you, Piper. I don't want her to be afraid of anything here."

"Thanks, Lance. I appreciate that." Piper sent up a quick prayer over this new day and this new father who was trying in the very best way.

* * *

Around four o'clock, the work truck crested the road, and Piper immediately saw the copper hair of her daughter in the cab. She hurried out of the booth and stood on the roadside, waving as soon as she caught Maelyn's attention.

Lance parked the truck and hopped out, allowing Maelyn to crawl out of his side of the truck.

"Mommy!" She ran up and threw her arms around Piper's waist. "Guess what?"

"What?"

"My new daddy said we could build a gazebo of my dreams!"

Piper hooked an eyebrow as she assessed Lance in the moment. Those blue eyes, dark lashes and the thought of a gazebo caused her heart to beat as if a first kiss were in store…

He offered a shadow of a smile and dipped his chin. "Will be second place to Grandpa Jo's." Did he wink? His gaze steadied on Maelyn. "Seems like an idyllic piece for a pumpkin patch, anyway."

"I get to help, too." Maelyn let go of Piper and stood next to Lance. "Can I go with…" She peered up at the giant orchard keeper. He was broad and tall—more akin to the Jolly Green Giant than an Iowa produce manager. "What should I call you, by the way?"

Piper suppressed a giggle and marveled at this glorious glimpse of her daughter casting off the shy shell in front of her father.

Lance shifted his weight and locked eyes with Piper. "Uh, I would love to be called Daddy." He then turned to Maelyn and crouched down, facing her. "But only when you are ready. I know this is very new. We have all the time in the world."

Maelyn tapped her chin, then patted Lance's shoulder like she would when comforting Piper. Maelyn ran up to Piper again. "Can I go with Mr. Lance to the store to get the stuff for the gazebo?"

"Sure. As long as he grabs your booster seat from my car."

Maelyn tossed a fist in the air as if she'd won a race, then ran over to the truck. "Let's go see the pumpkin patch. Come on, Mr. Lance." Piper refrained from dropping her mouth. Maelyn was brighter than ever. Piper should have never hidden her existence. She inhaled a choppy breath. There was that tweak of regret again.

"Okay, okay," Lance conceded with amusement. But after he helped her into the truck then slid behind the steering wheel, Piper spied a shadow cross his face just like the one that hovered over her conscience. Lance had done nothing wrong, though. She approached his open window and handed him her keys. He took them without looking at her.

"Everything okay?" Piper didn't want him to say anything negative around Maelyn. "She's super excited to do this with you, Lance."

"That's *Mr. Lance*, to you." His sneer-turned-smile was still a sneer after all. "*Daddy* would be appropriate," he whispered.

"It takes time, remember?" Piper observed Maelyn from the corner of her eye. She had her arms folded on the open window, admiring the hayride stop decked out with hay bales and pumpkins along the fence.

Lance's blue gaze captured Piper's with a flash of anguish. Her daughter's father was broken because of Piper's reckless decision. Because of her own fear.

Was it worth it now, after all she'd been through, to hold him back in a different way than before—not his college career, but his dream of fatherhood? And, more sobering, to stall a happy childhood for her daughter for so many years? If Piper sat in that for very long, she'd crawl out of her skin. She had never considered the positive effect Lance had on Maelyn. How could she have known?

At the obvious change in her daughter's countenance, Piper was certain that Lance would get all he dreamed of as a father. As a mother, she couldn't help but thank God for something stirring inside her more and more—hope.

They settled into a routine the rest of the week. Janet and Amelia met Maelyn at her bus stop, then walked her to Lance in the production area. Maelyn was a helper for Lance wherever he went around the property. Each night, she would share all about her day with Piper— how she'd used some tools with Lance's supervision, how she was able to pick some little pumpkins for Marge's pumpkin pie or how she had the whole corn pool to herself at closing time. And each night, Piper wrestled with a bittersweet niggle in her conscience. Her daughter was thriving now. That was all that mattered.

The Friday afternoon before the harvest festival, Sidney insisted that Piper join Lance and Maelyn to package the baskets they would donate.

"Come on, Piper. You have been cooped up in your booth while your daughter runs around the place. It will be fun."

"Does Lance think so?"

"He is over the moon. You should hear him talk about Maelyn at dinner. She's got him wrapped around her little finger."

Piper swallowed away rising emotion. "Well, that's sweet."

"You've pretty much made his dream come true."

"Well, I can attest to him making my dream come true."

Sidney raised her eyebrow.

"Maelyn has never been so happy in her life. This is why I left Waterloo. I wish I had known. Mae wouldn't have had such a rocky childhood—" She pressed her lips together at her confession.

"Hey, there." Sidney wrapped her in a hug. "All things work for our good…according to His purpose," Sidney regurgitated a Bible verse their old youth group leader would say. "You all are where you should be now. That's what counts. Come on. I'll drive you down."

A cold breeze caught the gold and red leaves that had just started to color the landscape. They tumbled across the road as the women hopped in the truck.

"Starting to feel like Harvest Festival weather. I wish the pumpkin patch were ready," Sidney said as they started down the road. "Our grand opening has been pushed back a few days. We'll open next Wednesday instead, since Lance insisted on that gazebo."

Had anyone ever been so enthralled with her little girl? "He's a sweet guy."

Sidney gave her a sideways glance. "Oh? You see it, too? Why'd you two break up, anyway?"

Piper kept an eye on the light bouncing off the metal roof ahead. "We hadn't really talked about what would happen when he went to college. The thrill of a secret relationship, when we'd pretty much grown up with everyone knowing our business in small-town Iowa, was exciting—for both of us. And I'd had a crush on him for quite a while." Sidney gasped but Piper continued, "While you were at camp, he took me fishing at the old pond down the way one night. We talked and talked.

He shared how nervous he was about going to school, and I shared the ultimatum my stepdad had given me. Pay rent or move out. We both had all these what-ifs ahead. The only sure thing seemed to be when we were together. He was honest and considerate, and I realized how much I respected him—how much I had admired him beyond our silly squabbles." She softly laughed. "He seemed to see me as someone totally different than what everyone saw."

"What do you mean? Not the spunky wild child? If I recall, that's close to Lance's description of you."

"Not that. He told me I was valued. That I was a light—in his life."

Sidney leaned back. "Did he really say that? Whoa, he was always so much more mature than we were."

"Hadn't thought of it in a long time." Piper turned away and looked out the window at the customers unloading from the hayride. "It got messy so quickly."

"Keep an open mind, Piper. Messes can be cleaned up. Just give him time."

"Funny—I said the same thing to him. Give Maelyn time to warm up. She sure has."

Sidney laughed. "She's definitely attached. Look." She pointed over to the opened garage door. Lance was giving Maelyn a piggyback ride around the production area. All the while, Maelyn's head was tossed back with belly-shaking laughter.

"She's a Hudson when she laughs." Sidney opened her door. "A Hudson through and through."

Piper couldn't help but smile. She was happy for her little girl. Piper had longed to be a Hudson when she had been the only girl with Gray for a last name. Now her daughter had inherited that dream come true. Making that happen was the least a mother could do.

## Chapter Seventeen

Lance's side hurt after galloping around. His daughter was making up for lost time, it seemed. The past week was all he'd ever hoped for in being a father. Teaching a little Hudson about the family business, observing that sense of awe and excitement in the small stuff, realizing that he could offer joy to someone without any expectation of something in return. Maelyn brightened his life more than he'd ever imagined a person could. He shook off the familiarity of it all. He'd once considered Piper a light that nobody could outshine.

Maelyn was a person who would always be in his life—like any other Hudson. After the last year of being cut off from a relationship with Tara, then realizing that he had been purposely cut out of life with Piper all this time—well, Maelyn had given him security that there was still trustworthy goodness in this world. That maybe, Lance had been given a gift after all the heartache. More than once, he couldn't help but whisper a shaky prayer of thanks.

He pulled out the rolling cart filled with the baskets they were going to prep for the women's shelter. As he positioned it near the discard bin, he noticed Piper and Sidney walking up.

"Hey, Lance. Piper's going to help you all get those baskets ready."

"Not going to take too long. They only have eight women at the shelter right now."

Maelyn held up an apple. "What about this one?" Her little hand cradled an apple like it was a treasure.

"Looks good, sweetheart. That brown mark is only there because it rubbed against the tree too much."

Maelyn lifted her chin with obvious Hudson pride and placed the apple in one of the baskets.

"First one down," Piper exclaimed as she wrapped her arm around her daughter's shoulder and gave her a kiss on the temple.

"Mr. Lance, what's a shelter?"

Piper opened her mouth to speak, but Lance answered, "It's a place for women who don't have a home yet."

Maelyn's forehead wrinkled upward, and she stuck her tongue in the space where teeth were just growing in. "Like a hotel?"

Piper gave a nervous laugh. "Exactly, Maelyn. Now, let's find another almost perfect apple." She began to rummage through the produce. Lance steadied his curiosity about Piper's nervousness and admired the mother and child before him. Their red hair and ivory skin were a perfect match. Piper's petite face was her own, while Maelyn's more round face favored his family.

As they worked side by side, he quietly observed Piper and Maelyn's relationship. Nurture exuded Piper's every movement and tone. The humor-laden woman discarded sarcasm for sweet affirmations to their daughter.

When the first basket was filled, Piper stepped back

and placed her hands on her hips. But unlike the last time she'd taken this stance—across from Lance with anger clearly pulsating in her blotchy neck right before they'd told his parents—she beamed pure affection toward the little girl. "You are quite the apple picker, Miss Orchard."

Maelyn did a wobbly dance back and forth with her shoulders and licked her bottom lip. Her happy gaze landed on Lance. "Did I do good, Da—Mr. Lance?"

What was that? Had she almost called him Daddy? Oh, Lance's heart flipped over and over. He couldn't wait to hear that name spoken about him. "Uh, you sure did. I think your mama's right. Miss Orchard is a perfect title for you."

Maelyn smiled so big, then stepped off the step stool she'd been using. "Is it okay if I go to the bathroom, though?"

Piper snickered and grabbed her hand. "Even Miss Orchard needs to step away to powder her nose every once in a while." Maelyn gave her a confused look. Piper said, "Yes, you can go to the bathroom, Mae. I'll take you."

Maelyn wiggled her hand out of Piper's. "I know where it is, Mom." She skipped across the production area.

Piper hurried after her, catching the door as Maelyn disappeared out the front to the public restrooms on the other side of the café. "I'll wait right here, Mae." She glanced over and caught him staring. Tension tightened his every muscle, and he looked away.

"She's really grown comfortable around here." Piper shoved her hands in her pockets as she leaned against the open door.

"Yep," is all Lance could manage.

"I... I... I just want to thank you for being a good dad to her."

Lance paused sorting through the apples. His eyes blurred. But he couldn't think of anything not begrudging to say back. He wasn't proud of the way the sour feeling sat at the back of his throat whenever Piper was around.

She continued, "Also, thank you for following through with giving those apples to women in need."

Lance gave a curt smile. "It was a good idea."

Piper stared outside, her teeth pressing on her bottom lip. "Maelyn and I were at that shelter once...when she was about two."

His hunch was right. He stepped away from his work and crossed over. Mirroring Piper, he shoved his hands in his pockets and leaned on the counter across from her. "What happened?"

A bitter smile crept along her face. "Garrett had left. I couldn't get ahold of him for a couple days. He had the credit card and the car. I needed groceries. He'd forgotten to pay the electricity bill. It...it was a dark time—literally." An unamused laugh puffed from her lips.

A million questions tamped down all the resentment Lance felt earlier. "How did you get to Rapid Falls? And why didn't you go to your mom's?" *Or here—my parents would have helped you in a heartbeat.*

"One of Garrett's friends showed up looking for him to go to a concert in Des Moines. He agreed to drop Maelyn and me off at Mom's on the way. But Mom was out of town and there was no way to get inside." Piper inhaled deeply and continued, "So, Maelyn and I had a pretend bear hunt straight to the steps of the newly opened women's shelter. It's a safe house for women to escape from the cities of their..." Her face blanched. She turned her head quickly and flashed a smile at Maelyn, who skipped through the door.

She placed her hands on both of Maelyn's shoulders and followed behind her all the way to the baskets. "I know for a fact that the need is great, and these baskets will be much appreciated."

As Lance joined them, anger threatened to crumble his stoic demeanor toward Piper. But she wasn't the object causing him to see red more vibrant than the apples they inspected. Garrett was the last guy that Lance would have struck up a conversation with during high school, and now he'd be the first guy Lance would confront if he could. What kind of man abandons his wife and little girl with no money or food? Piper didn't say how long she'd been at the shelter, or how she'd ended up enduring five more years with someone so neglectful. Lance wasn't so sure he wanted to find out.

The torment of knowing what Piper and Maelyn might have gone through was greater than knowing his own ex-wife was happily making home with someone else.

Piper maintained a consistent work ethic as they finished up the baskets. She'd spilled her guts to Lance to back up her appreciation for the way he treated Maelyn, but now she'd opened a different door besides the one to the metal building—a door into her miserable existence before.

She investigated the surface of the fruit. The blemishes were specks compared to the fruit's value. Still worth keeping. The choice to move forward, blemish and all, was the best thing Piper could have done. Look at Maelyn now. Smiling and bright. The mistake of choosing Garrett for husband material was as obvious as the bruise on the apple she now held, especially when Lance Hudson had every right to be in the running. Ack! Heat raced up her neck and flooded her cheeks with fire.

Husband material? What was she thinking? He was father material.

*That's what I meant*, she chided herself over and over.

"Looks like we are just about done." Lance stretched his back.

Maelyn jumped from the stepping stool to the floor with a thump. "Yay. Can we go to the parade now?"

"First thing in the morning, Mae." Piper wiped her hands on her jeans. "Why don't we go home and see Grandma?"

"Or how about I buy you all dinner?" Lance offered. "I am dropping off some pies to the Rapid Falls diner. I have been craving their tenderloin all day." He flashed a smile at his daughter. "The sandwich is probably as big as your face, Maelyn. You should see it."

Maelyn clutched at Piper's arm. "Mommy, can we go?"

"Uh, well…" Piper wanted to say, *Are you sure you want me there?* But Lance didn't seem inauthentic in his invitation in any way. She was the one that was known to withhold the truth of the matter.

Maelyn was practically begging, hanging on her arm and bouncing on her toes.

Piper mouthed to Lance, "You sure?"

He nodded with not one speck of hesitation.

"I guess… I can follow you in my car."

Maelyn protested, wanting them to ride together.

Lance suggested, "Why don't I drive, and I can bring your car tomorrow morning before the parade? We can just ride to the parade together, and then I can get a ride home with Dad." He gaped playfully at Maelyn. "As long as it doesn't rain."

"Sure. Sounds good."

Maelyn squealed and ran to the door. "I want to measure my face to that sandwich Mr. Lance talked about."

Lance and Piper both laughed then walked with Maelyn. Lance headed to the café to grab the pies and met them at his truck.

Piper didn't really want to think anymore. She chose to live vicariously through her daughter—enjoying a date to Rapid Falls Diner with her daddy…and her mom tagging along.

## Chapter Eighteen

Lance spied Maelyn through the rearview mirror with nervous repetition, distracting himself from the beauty sitting next to him. No matter what poor decision Piper had made in the past, after spending this afternoon witnessing her love for Maelyn, Lance wanted to be part of whatever this was. A family? Not quite. But somehow, their daughter made his future brighter than he could ever imagine, and that drew Lance closer to Piper than he cared to admit. He needed Piper Gray. If only as the mother who'd cared exceptionally well for his daughter. And while he wasn't thrilled about needing Piper, he was somehow at peace with it. If only he could convince his heart to slow down and accept this arrangement as purely platonic. Lance wasn't ready to give his heart away to someone who'd already cast it aside once.

"Do you still go fishing out at the pond?" Piper offered a reprieve from the silence. His chest warmed and tightened all at once. She was the only other person who knew about his fishing spot. He hadn't shared that secret place with anyone else.

"Not for years." He inhaled. "You were with me the last time I fished there."

Piper glanced over at him. "Oh, really?"

"Yep, best kept secret." Lance grimaced. Poor choice of words with this woman. He reached over and turned on the radio to an oldies station.

They passed Jim's grocery and Nonny's retirement center, then turned onto the quaint streetscape of Main. Round barrels dotted along the wide sidewalks, spilling with gold mums and trailing ivy. Eclectic storefronts lined the street, each facade with its own flair depending on the color of awning, the addition of shutters and the unique window stylings. Two city blocks of colorful planters, old-fashioned streetlamps and booming small-town business. As always. Lance had delivered pies to the Rapid Falls Diner since he first started driving, and he had frequented the handful of restaurants whenever he was home from college.

He parallel parked in front of the diner and put some quarters in the meter while Piper helped Maelyn down from the truck. Lance grabbed the box of pies, then they headed inside.

The usual savory scent of buttery grilled hamburger buns filled the restaurant. Wood-paneled walls were decked out in the same Rapid Falls Eagles gear that colored Lance's high school days. A flag with the high school mascot—an eagle wearing pilot goggles—and several jerseys from various sports boasting the green and white of RFHS covered the walls and screamed "Go Eagles Go" in his memory.

The place was buzzing with conversation. Lance took the pies to the kitchen, and Piper found a booth. Maelyn clung close to her mother's leg. Some kids were just shy, but Lance had a sneaking suspicion that life before had given his daughter some insecurity. His heart grew heavy, and he tried to focus on his task.

When he returned from the kitchen, he spotted Piper and Maelyn sitting in a booth by the old jukebox, peering at the laminated menu together. On a deep inhale of home-cooked goodness, Lance headed to join them just as the waitress approached with waters.

"We know what we want, Lance. I think you do, too?" Piper handed her menu to the waitress.

"Uh, yep. Ladies first." He smiled at Maelyn.

Piper said, "She'll have the tenders basket, and I'll have the garden salad with a cup of baked-potato soup."

"That's it, Piper? They have dinners on the other side of the menu."

She just shook her head and gave a tight smile. "I'm fine."

Lance lifted his brows then handed over his menu. He didn't need to look. "I'll have the number five with a side of mashed potatoes."

"Will that be all?"

Lance leaned over to Maelyn. "Do you like cheese curds?"

Maelyn's brow crinkled, and she shifted her eyes in Piper's direction.

"She'll try anything." Piper took a sip of her water.

Lance studied her. She didn't look at him, only focused on her drink. He couldn't help but think about Piper mentioning their food insecurity with Garrett. If there was one thing he remembered about Piper, it was her absolute love for cheese curds.

"An order of cheese curds, please." Lance winked at Maelyn. "You will love them. Sometimes, they will squeak when you bite into them."

Maelyn wrinkled her nose. "Like a mouse?"

Lance chuckled. "No, like…" He shrugged his shoulders. "Like a cheese curd. One of the things I missed while living out west."

Maelyn swiveled in her seat as a man approached the jukebox. He put a couple quarters in and pressed his selection. An old country song began to play. Maelyn turned around again.

"Did that man make the song play?"

"Yes. It's a jukebox. Wanna go pick a song?" Lance dug into his pockets for quarters.

Piper scooted out of the seat and pulled some change out of her pocket. "I got it, Lance." She handed Maelyn the quarters. "You want me to help you?"

"No, I want to surprise you." Maelyn huffed as she moved out of the booth, then whispered, "Just stand right there, Mom."

His little girl headed to the other side of the booth where the jukebox sat.

"Can she read the songs?" Lance wondered.

"Oh, yeah. She's an advanced reader. We read all the time when she was little."

"That's good." Lance stirred his ice water with his straw. "I am really impressed with you, Piper."

Piper's lips parted and she cocked her head in question. "Are you being sarcastic?"

He smiled. "No, I am serious. You have such a way with her." They both glanced over at Maelyn. "And I am so sorry about what you went through."

Piper shifted from one foot to the other, her brow furrowing as she lowered her eyes. "I am really sorry, too."

"I hope to drown out any sour memories for Maelyn with a lifetime of sweet ones." A faint smile released Piper's tense look. "And I guess I will give you a chance, too."

Her green eyes darted up and locked him in an expectant stare.

Suddenly, heat flashed across his chest. "Give you a chance to share in those sweet memories. You know, as the mom." He winked, even though there was nothing he felt that was humorous. What he said did not match the welling anticipation of all that he could give Piper Gray, if he didn't have such a track record of falling so deeply only to be trampled upon.

"Piper? I thought I recognized you." Della Carson, their old youth group leader, called from a booth and walked over to them. "Janet mentioned you were back. How have you been?"

"Better than ever." Piper flashed a bright smile.

"Oh, well, that's good." Della chuckled and squeezed Lance's shoulder. "I know these Hudsons have helped you out over the years. When I heard you were back and working at the orchard, I worried you were in some sort of trouble."

Piper's forehead tweaked with hurt for a split-second, then she reengaged her happiest grin. "Nope, no trouble."

"She's like family, Della." He didn't like seeing the subtle discomfort in Piper's expression.

"That's nice," Della cooed. "Your parents are so generous, Lance. Always giving to those who need it most. Can't believe their donation to the Fall Festival this year."

"Janet and Don are the best. We'll see you around, Della," Piper exclaimed.

Della said goodbye and wove her way back to her table.

Piper watched Maelyn finishing up her selection. Della had added a weird tension to the air, and implied that Piper was needy. The woman didn't know that Piper had chosen a women's shelter over the Hudsons. That Piper was the one who'd tried to cut ties with his family to give Lance the chance to follow his own dream. Had Lance ever held someone's future in his hands? Piper had stepped back for his future, and now she had her little girl to sacrifice for. He could only rise to the challenge of insisting Piper wasn't alone in that sacrifice.

"I think she has the wrong impression—you weren't a burden on my family." Lance's heart skipped when Piper looked his way again. "They liked helping you out." She opened her mouth to speak, but Maelyn returned. Piper moved out of the way as Maelyn crawled into their booth again.

Piper plopped down on a sigh. "So, Mae, what song did you choose?"

"You'll see…or hear." She did her little wobble dance where she moved back and forth and beamed with pride. Lance heard her heels kicking against the booth.

The waitress arrived with their plates of food. "Thank you." His mouth watered but his stomach was in knots.

"It *is* as big as my face!" Maelyn pressed forward staring at the breaded tenderloin sticking out beneath the bun.

Lance held up his sandwich between them. "Yep. And I am going to eat every last bit. But first, a cheese curd."

They dug in, enjoying the squeaky cheese. He was happy to see Piper partake as well. If there was one thing Lance would make sure of, it was that his daughter and her mother would never go hungry again.

Maelyn gasped. "Listen!"

A country ballad tumbled out of the machine behind the two redheads, and the lyrics began. Something about daddy and love and being there for the hard times.

"I chose it for you, Mr. Lance." Maelyn munched on a cheese curd. "It's called Daddy…uh…something. I just remember *Daddy* was in it."

"Thank you, sweetheart." Lance forced a smile. Conflict raged within him—awakened sorrow for missing out on his daughter's life, but unthinkable gratitude for the amazing gift in Maelyn.

Piper reached over and covered his hand with hers. "Thank you for dinner, Lance. One sweet memory to add to her list." She smirked, but her eyes rounded in sincerity. He couldn't help but hope she'd add this memory to her own list also.

Piper and Maelyn headed outside while Lance paid the check. The rest of Main was lit up with streetlamps and glowing shop windows—mainly restaurants and boutiques. Chalkboard signs advertised harvest specials, and couples and families traversed the sidewalks on either side of the car-lined street.

Fall was in the air. Crisp, smoky-scented air and a slight chill encouraged wrapping in a blanket and sipping cocoa—or cider. Piper hadn't enjoyed the seasons in a long time. Finally, she had permission to go where she wanted, when she wanted and, in the meantime, just be a human in creation, enjoying it fully. And this evening was near perfect—except Della had implied Piper was known as the troubled one needing help around here.

Lance joined them outside and opened both doors for Piper and Maelyn, then drove them home.

"Thank you, Mr. Lance." Maelyn crawled out of the back seat. Piper helped her down.

"Thanks, Lance. It was nice of you to treat us." Piper closed Maelyn's door.

The passenger window rolled down, and Lance called out, "Piper?"

She stepped to the open window.

"If you ever want to do this again, I would love it. Taking you all out to dinner has been a highlight for me."

Piper leaned on the window. "Maelyn would love that."

"Would you?" He splayed his hand on the passenger seat and leaned forward. "I meant the three of us."

How could any woman deny Lance Hudson's offer to take her out to dinner? He was a perfect gentleman, a tender father and the definition of trustworthy. What was it about Lance that made her want to set up a dinner for three every night far into the future? He was someone she'd never expected to come alongside her in this journey alone with Maelyn.

What might have life been like if he'd been beside her all this time?

Their encounter with Della pinched her thoughts.

"Thank you, Lance. We'll try to make it work."

He tipped his hat, and Piper stepped away from the window, her emotions tumbling like leaves in an autumn spiral. She had come so far—leaving Garrett, getting Maelyn into counseling and working. But Della had seen Piper the way Piper had seen herself back then—maybe the real reason she'd never told Lance about the pregnancy test. She had looked up to those Hudsons so much, and in doing that, she'd viewed herself as inferior. The difference between Hudson and Gray was as clear as an Iowa October sky. They were a solid family with a successful business. Her family had been unstable and trying to make ends meet. She had been so worried that she'd mess everything up by admitting the pregnancy to them. She had cowered to her insecurity and look what had happened.

No more.

Piper knew better now. She had been determined to help herself and not depend on anyone once she'd left Garrett. Why was it so easy to lean into Sidney, Janet, Don and especially Lance?

As Piper followed Maelyn inside her mom's house, she flashed back to the days when she would come home only if Mom's ex-husband was at work or out of town. The open invitation to the Hudsons was more a lure away from the dim existence that was an ironic truth for life as a Gray. Mom added color of her own when her husband was away, ordering pizza and watching chick flicks with Piper, trying her best to keep the shadows at bay.

"Mommy, can I sleep with you tonight?" Maelyn snuggled against Piper's leg as they traipsed through the dark living room. Piper clicked on a lamp. Mom's jacket and Bill's coat were gone. They must still be at work, or maybe they had gone out to eat also. It was Friday night, after all.

"Why don't we get our PJs on and cuddle on the couch? We can have a movie night."

Maelyn perked up and skipped ahead. "Yay!" Her long red braids swung back and forth.

Gray existence wasn't dim anymore, and Piper was independent as much as she could manage. These things took time, she thought, as she walked the hallway to her old room. Maelyn had a place to go after school now, and while Lance was willing to give Piper more hours, she couldn't help but take her mother's advice at last.

It was time for Piper to fully activate her plan for life after marriage. She needed a solid job—and that was one thing Hudson Orchard couldn't provide.

## Chapter Nineteen

Before Lance drove home, he detoured to the old fishing pond that Piper had mentioned. He had hoped to own land near his family just like this. When he married Tara, he thought they were on the same page. Build a resume, work hard, then come back and settle down. They seemed to hold the same future, hand in hand.

Lance parked, stepped onto unkempt grass and walked over to the old dock. The moonlight shimmered on the water. Tonight had been the closest thing to fulfilling his dream for family. And he'd meant it when he'd invited Piper to join in future meals, regardless of the hitch in his spirit to guard his heart. Could he fully trust Piper Gray again?

Lance peered up at the sky glittering with stars. Trust had been more an enemy than a friend these past few years. Trust was like this sparkling dark water turning to a mirage by the light of day. He suspected, though, that this water was the real thing—just like the love he felt for a daughter he hardly knew.

Lance sighed, then walked over to his truck and drove home.

Sidney pulled into the driveway just as Lance got out of his truck.

"Hey, sis, how were the in-laws?" He helped her with the infant carrier.

"Good. We all video-called with Todd." Her hushed voice indicated Amelia was sleeping. They climbed the porch stairs.

Lance lowered his voice, too. "That's good. Hope he's doing well."

Her relaxed smile and nod meant she felt confident he was safe and sound overseas.

"I am glad you don't have to worry about him. Just a few more weeks, right?"

"Yep. Can't wait." She held open the front door for Lance. "Where've you been?"

"To dinner with Maelyn and Piper."

"Really?" Sidney took the baby carrier and set it gently in the dark living room, then headed to the kitchen and grabbed a glass of water. "How was it?"

Lance followed her and sat on a stool. "Honestly?" Sidney paused and arched her eyebrows. "It was nearly perfect."

Her smile grew wide. She set the glass on the counter. "Really?"

"How many times are you going to say that?" Lance chuckled. "Doesn't sound like they've eaten out much. Garrett seems like a tyrant." He clenched his jaw. "Maelyn deserves a good father."

"And you are the second best," she quipped. "Todd and Dad tie for first place." They both laughed. "Seriously, Lance. I have been so in awe of you with Maelyn. And I am glad that you and Piper are getting along, too."

"We're going to be part of each other's lives for a long while." Lance swallowed hard, pulling back the reigns on his overactive pulse. "I mean, as parents to Maelyn. That's all."

Sidney's blue eyes simmered. "I never understood what she saw in Garrett—especially after you told me what happened between you two. Piper crushed on you for so long."

"She told you that?"

"I only suspected… She kind of confirmed it at our last sleepover before I went away to work that summer." Sidney sat on the stool next to Lance. "Which makes sense now. She would always joke about you following me around until I got married, and I—" She narrowed her eyes and bit her lip. "Well, I kinda blew it off with a negative comment about your overprotectiveness."

"Oh, thanks." Lance gave a teasing frown. "She's never let me live that down."

"But I knew she cared for you, Lance, because she took me by the shoulders and made me promise something." Sidney shook her head, and muttered, "I can't believe I forgot."

"What?"

"She made me promise to never take you for granted. How blessed I was to have someone in my life who cared so much. And how she hoped you cared for her, too."

"I did. Probably realized it about that same time," Lance admitted. Sidney placed her hand over his. "If she cared for me so much, why would she go and choose a guy like Garrett?"

"You were taking off for college, and Garrett offered her the first chance to move out of her parents' house." Sidney furrowed her brow. "Guess if you are told you are a bother so much—like her stepdad said often— you won't think you deserve as much as the amazing brother of your best friend."

"But what we had together was so great, so real. To me, anyway."

"Do you think it could be that way again?" Sidney prodded, even though she casually sipped her water.

"Oh, we've both gone through so much. I think being good parents to Maelyn is the most important thing."

"You both show up here at the exact time, and she's got the daughter you've always dreamt of." Sidney set her glass down. "God has brought you all together for such a time as this."

Lance thought about the mirage of trust over the years. While he'd been burned a time or two, he marveled at Mae's trust in him so quickly. He would continue to be the one person she could trust, besides Piper. He was her father, after all. That was what good fathers did. His spirit swelled. If there was one person who deserved Lance's trust, it was his heavenly Father. "I haven't given God much credit. Always wondered why things didn't go my way. Blamed Him."

He would be devastated if Maelyn ever blamed him for being absent those years.

Sidney placed her hand on his arm. "He's always there for you, even when you blame Him for other people's choices."

"I know, Sid. Mom and Dad have modeled that well over the years. For us, and Piper."

Amelia started to whimper from the living room. Sidney scooted back and stood.

"I am sorry she never told you…or me…about Maelyn. But I am so glad you are both back now." She leaned over and kissed Lance on the cheek.

Lance headed upstairs, but before he got ready for bed, he pulled out his old Bible from high school. And college, it seemed, because the two letters he'd written to Piper from his dorm room were stuck in the back. He'd never sent them because he'd found out she was engaged shortly after he'd left.

What would have happened if she'd read them?

Had Piper felt the same for him back then as he had for her? It didn't really matter now.

Lance flipped open his Bible and read while a question formed in his heart.

Did God plant the seed of longing for a family last year, not because of some fictional chance with Tara, but because He knew all along the roots that were already growing in Iowa?

Before Maelyn woke up the next morning, Piper borrowed Mom's computer and began to look for jobs in the school districts around Rapid Falls. Not Rapid Falls CSD, though. After the awkwardness with Della, and knowing most of the staff hadn't changed, Piper-the-Great was just fine driving a little farther away.

Nonetheless, a school job would at least give her similar hours to Maelyn. And being a mom and a high school graduate gave her enough experience to be in the early-childhood classroom as an associate. She sketched out a schedule for Maelyn to visit her father but still have plenty of time with Piper. The arrangement looked good on paper. A smidge of peace lessened her conflicted allegiance to the Hudsons. If only Piper could move this all along immediately, surely peace in the fullest would follow. But for now, it was time to smile and wave from atop the hayride in the Harvest Parade.

They dressed and ate a quick breakfast, then stepped into the chilly first-of-October air.

"Bundle up, Mae." Piper adjusted Maelyn's buttoned-up corduroy coat and pulled her cute Rapid Falls Eagles knit stocking cap over her ears. "I remember wearing this hat when I was your age."

Maelyn searched her face with those pretty peridot eyes. "Can I have a hat with a big *H* on it like yours and Mr. Lance's?"

Piper tweaked her chin. "That's for work, and a baseball cap won't keep your head warm."

"But then everyone will know I belong there, too."

Piper knew the tug of longing to be a part of the Hudson family. At least Lance had admitted to Della that she was like family.

"Mae, you belong next to me and your dad—Mr. Lance. And we are the ones that count the most, right?" Piper giggled and kissed her nose. "Oh, my, your nose is freezing!" But Piper's anticipation warmed her whole chest. Piper, Lance and Maelyn sitting together on the hay bales was less of a work-related arrangement and more of an unexpected family affair—one that stirred up a different longing within Piper. And it had nothing to do with wishing she lived on Hudson land and everything to do with wishing she belonged beside Lance in a way that was once a brimming hope, then a dream come true that had ended much too quickly.

Lance carefully turned Piper's sedan into the driveway so as to not spill the steaming cider in to-go cups. Maelyn and Piper were sitting on the front steps, cuddled under a fleece blanket. They were picture–perfect, as far as Lance was concerned. He hardly slept last night but prayed about the possibility that a hand much bigger than his was at work. He read the letters he'd written to Piper over and over again. They belonged to the girl who was under the impression that she didn't deserve a guy like him, according to Sidney.

If Piper had any inkling of that lie remaining, after all that Garrett had put her through, then those letters were a gift she needed to receive. But too much of Lance's lovesickness seeped through what he'd written. He should just throw them away. Instead, he'd tucked them back in his Bible.

"Good morning," he said, trying to not wake up the neighborhood. It was only seven on a Saturday.

Maelyn sprung from the steps and ran to the car while Piper folded up the blanket and followed behind her.

"Hi, Mr. Lance." Maelyn hugged him, and Lance kissed the top of her knit cap.

"Hello, sweetheart. Ready to go?" He opened the back seat door for Maelyn, then handed Piper her keys.

"Oh, thanks." Piper's hands were frigid as she took the keys from him.

"Do you need gloves?" Lance refrained from taking her hand and warming it with his own.

"I couldn't find mine. I have pockets, though." She smiled and slipped past him to get to the driver's side.

Lance took off his gloves. "Here, Piper. There's no reason to be miserable."

"What about you?" She ogled at his gloves that were probably two sizes too big.

"Don't worry about me." Seriously, she should not worry about Lance. He didn't want any more of this deserving versus undeserving idea. He was desperate to move on from the brain fog that this woman induced in him.

"Okay." She smiled once again. "Thanks, Lance." Piper tossed her keys on the driver's seat then pulled on the gloves. She held each hand beside her cheeks, the fingers of the gloves folding over. "Or should I call you

Giant Lance?" Her giggle was too pleasant for a man who was trying to remain focused. How would he manage to keep his attention on his daughter alone, when her mama would beam and smile and joke whenever she was near? How'd he managed to leave her behind for Stanford? He had found out that Piper and Garrett had reconciled the day before his flight to California. He'd never had the gumption to turn plans upside down. He played things safe. And he'd shrunk back from allowing his heart to take the lead from his good sense.

He glimpsed past the floppy gloves at the little girl in the back seat. If he had known about the pregnancy, would he have left? Maybe not. Or would he have taken Piper with him? Yet, another thought crept into his mind. Maybe, just maybe, God had ordained a life without maybes—only eventuallys. *Eventually*, they'd made it here together. And everything seemed to work out for the best—for the little girl who needed a dad, and the man who needed a family.

He loped around the front of the car, determined to outpace the last sentiment. His family was waiting for him in the Rapid Falls commerce area. Waiting for him and the newest member of the Hudson tree. That was the family he needed. Nobody else could fill that. Nobody else was as loyal and steady as a Hudson.

"Mr. Lance, is that cup for me?" Maelyn bounced her heel off the car seat and had her gloved hands folded in her lap.

"It sure is. The Maelyn special." He sat down, lifted the kid-size cup from the back seat cupholder and gave it to Maelyn.

"The Maelyn special?" Piper's voice dripped with her usual snark.

"Cider with two ice cubes." He winked at Piper, regretting it immediately as her skin flushed almost as instantly. That loving gesture was meant for his daughter.

Or was it?

He couldn't help but revel in the old affection that bumbled around his heart at Piper's beauty.

*Okay, your cool-as-an-autumn-day starts now.*

Lance turned around and buckled his seatbelt while Piper began to back down the driveway.

"I take it that one of those is for me?" Piper spoke through whatever blush he'd seemingly activated.

"Of course. Hospitality is our middle name."

She slid a look to him. "*H* is for…"

"Hudson!" Maelyn called out.

They all laughed. Lance splayed his hands on his jeans and looked out the window at the golds, greens and browns of the tree-lined street, praying that he could fully accept the changes in his life along with the shifting season.

Piper parallel parked along the side street of the women's shelter. "This way we can leave after we deliver the apples." She glanced in the rearview mirror, wondering if Maelyn had any recollection of this place. They had only stayed a week when she was two.

Lance was already out on the sidewalk opening the passenger door for Maelyn by the time Piper grabbed her purse and her keys.

"Come on, Miss Orchard. Let's go find the hayride." He held her hand like Maelyn was royalty—his palm up, hers holding a gentle grasp. Piper almost expected him to bow. Maelyn giggled and hopped up on her sneakered feet, grabbing on to Lance's arm with both hands. There was nothing sweeter than hearing her daughter's glee. Piper swallowed hard and joined them on the sidewalk.

"Let's go find Grandpa Hudson!" Maelyn said. "Oh, I forgot my cider."

"I'll get it—" Piper and Lance spoke almost in unison and leaned toward the door.

Lance stepped back. "Ladies first." He did bow then. In a stiff, uncomfortable way—as if he were going to be playful but had caught his words before his movement.

Piper dipped her head, feeling absolutely conflicted by the sudden reaction within her. Her heart galloped, initiated too quickly by the charming guy whose spicy aftershave warmed the vicinity of their unloading zone. And that gold fleece sweatshirt setting his blue eyes ablaze with their amber specks didn't help.

Piper hesitated in the quiet safe haven of her car, grabbed the to-go cup, then exhaled upon returning to reality.

He was Maelyn's knight in shining armor...not Piper's.

"Mommy, you hold my cup just a little longer, I've always wanted to try this—" Maelyn's little tongue stuck out to one side, and she focused on her hand reaching for Lance's, then turned and wiggled her fingers to Piper's. Both Lance and Piper held onto their daughter's hands. "I saw my friend at school do this with her mommy and daddy. They swung their arms together and she jumped so high." Maelyn's face was bright. Lance's gaze crashed into Piper's. Was that pity or sympathy?

Piper knew her daughter hadn't ever been swung like most every other kid around here. A product of a marriage where one parent wasn't around for the walks and playtime. The fact that Maelyn had observed this was gut-wrenching.

"Well, now you get to be part of her firsts," Piper said to Lance. And if there were anyone in the world that Piper would want to be around for Maelyn's firsts, it was Lance Hudson. He was staring at her. "About time, right?" Piper smirked his way, trying to ignore a wave of sorrow for her daughter's father.

Lance's chest puffed out on an intake of breath and deflated on a stuttering sigh. He then commanded, "One, two, three," and together, they swung their arms backward then forward, launching Maelyn with a little help from her eager jump.

She squealed with delight. "Again! Again!"

Piper shrugged at Lance.

"Are you sure, Maelyn?" he teased.

"Yesss!" Her lisp was as loud as it had ever been. They swung her over and over until they reached the corner of Main.

The spectators for the parade already lined the street, crowding against the bay windows of shops and restaurants.

"Looks like we'd better hurry." Lance adjusted his hand to a firm grip of Maelyn's, and they snaked past some folks, crossed the street, then hurried into the neighborhood. "Dad's meeting us by the creamery."

They began to jog. Maelyn ran ahead. The creamery was owned by a local farmer and sold the best ice cream in the county. Piper's mom bought her milk from the creamery instead of the grocery store, and on occasion, they would splurge and buy grass-fed beef, too. This was Piper's favorite part of town—where idyllic small-town commerce spilled into the historic neighborhood of Rapid Falls. Pointed Victorian roofs and wraparound porches sat on sprawling lots. The creamery was sandwiched between two smaller houses-turned-small-businesses—one a hair salon and the other a veterinarian's office.

Don met Maelyn at the steps and helped her up onto

a hay bale next to Janet, Sidney and Amelia. Piper watched her daughter wiggle her way between her new aunt and grandmother. She grasped her baby cousin's hands that donned tiny mittens.

Don bounded down the steps. "Good morning, you two," he greeted in the most endearing mention of two very separate people as if they were one complete whole.

Piper felt like she was in high school all over again, picking up nonexistent signals as if the whole world revolved around her hopeful crushes.

The sun brightened as the trailer began to move. The Rapid Falls High School band was ahead of them, playing the school fight song as they marched down the street to the T-intersection of Main.

"Here you go, Mae." Sidney handed her a bucket of candy. Hearing Sidney use her nickname startled Piper. It was as if she'd always been part of their family. "Toss it to the other kids out there."

Maelyn turned around on her knees and pressed against the rail, dropping apple caramel lollipops and miniature nut rolls onto the road as kids swarmed against the outstretched arms of parents trying to keep them from getting too close to the vehicles.

Lance leaned over to Piper and muttered much too close to her ear, "She's a great kid, Piper. You've obviously done something right."

She turned to him, scooting back so as to not completely inhale every last delicious, Lance-scented particle of oxygen. "Well, thank you. She's obviously got a lot more growing to do—let's just hope the need to swing doesn't last too much longer." She rolled her shoulder, still feeling the strain from their recent stroll.

"Ah, we'll miss that." Lance nudged her with his shoulder.

*We'll.* There goes that clumping her with Lance Hudson again—by Lance himself this time. Piper settled back and enjoyed being part of the festivity.

At the end of the parade, they pulled up along the back entrance of the women's shelter. Maelyn belly-laughed as Lance scooped her up and gave her a piggyback ride down the steps.

"Come on, Piper." Sidney hooked arms with her. "Let's go get acquainted with the manager of RFWS. You know her, right?"

"Yep." *And so does Maelyn.* Piper shoveled in a deep breath of whatever air surrounded her—and Lance's cologne offered pleasant happenstance—because now she was Piper-the-Great, part two. Free from the pain that had pushed her here five years ago.

The manager, Brie Minter, seemed well trained on acting like a stranger to Piper. Being the matron of an emergency shelter like this branch of the larger inner-city shelter was a delicate position and needed extra precaution.

"Hey, Brie. It's okay. The Hudsons know we're friends." Piper squeezed the woman's arm. She was a vibrant lady with short white hair and thick, black-rimmed glasses. "I am so glad you allowed me to stay here, no questions asked." Brie relaxed and offered her usual friendly smile.

Piper could tell Sidney was gawking at her. Guess Lance hadn't filled her in on Piper's story.

Brie helped them unload the baskets and place them on a big metal cart in the center of the commercial kitchen. This place smelled like vanilla and window cleaner. A strange combination that meant security to Piper.

While Don and Brie arranged some future opportunities to help the shelter, Maelyn wandered into the dining room and knelt beside a laundry basket of toys. She glanced around the room, then locked eyes with Piper.

Piper hurried to her daughter and crouched down. "What is it, Mae?"

Maelyn ran her hand along the yarn hair of an old rag doll. "I had a toy just like this."

Piper picked up the doll. She remembered little Maelyn carrying it around these rooms and halls that week. "You played with this doll a long time ago. One day I will tell you about it." Piper handed her the doll. Maelyn examined it closely—the sewn patches on the dress, the fading smile printed on the cloth face—then gave the doll a kiss on the forehead and returned her to the basket. She scrambled to her feet and headed back through the kitchen to the trailer where Janet sat with Amelia. Lance and Sidney waited at the dining-room door.

Sidney crossed her arms and tilted her head as Piper approached them. "Why didn't you tell me?"

"What?" Piper stuck her hands in her back pockets. "That because of a bad choice I made, I couldn't feed my daughter properly?"

"Your choice?" Lance challenged. "I thought you said Garrett left you two without—"

"But it started with the choice to be with him in the first place. I know that now."

"You came all the way to Rapid Falls and didn't ask me for help?" Sidney's voice was hitched with hurt.

"You all had helped me enough, Sid. And besides, you were out of state." Was that the whole truth as to why she hadn't reached out to her best friend? Of course not. She had been hiding her daughter from the Hudsons for fear of the truth spilling out. "I—I was stuck."

Sidney let out a small huff. "You know, Piper. There is never too much help when it comes to family. You should have learned that through all our years together. But I guess we've always been friends on your terms. You got to choose when to show up and when to disappear." Sidney shook her head. "That's not very honoring to those who were there to help you."

Piper narrowed her eyes. She sounded like Della and probably anyone else who saw Piper Gray on Hudson property. "You all did help me. But at some point, I needed to help myself. Don't you see, Sidney? I am known as the girl who the Hudsons help out. The one time I step out on my own, I reap the consequences of a bad marriage. Please don't question my choices back then. I am a whole new person. I am done being a charity case."

Lance pushed away from the doorjamb. "You are not a charity case, Piper—"

"I totally was—during high school, and then when I showed up here." Hot tears seared Piper's eyes as she glanced around the shelter. "But not anymore. I am so very glad that my little girl has you all to love on. But now, it's time for me to help myself. This is my official two weeks' notice." Piper pushed through the two siblings and headed out the back door, swiped at her cheeks, then swiveled on her heels and faced Lance and Sidney. "Thank you so much for helping me. Truly. I appreciate you all." They were the best of her past and present. But her future had to be all her own.

## Chapter Twenty

Maelyn was atop the hayride, singing to Amelia in Janet's lap.

"Hey, Maelyn. It's time to go home." Piper's voice reached the highest of pitches. Maelyn kissed the baby, and Janet kissed Maelyn. She scrambled over the hay bales and bounced down the trailer steps.

"Mommy, can we go to the orchard today?"

"Not today." She grabbed her daughter's hand, waved to Janet and quickly walked away.

"Piper!" Brie hurried to meet her at the corner. "You're leaving without a goodbye?" The spritely woman opened her arms for a hug. They embraced, then Brie leaned down and squeezed Maelyn. "You two have blossomed into fine young ladies."

"I am trying to take your advice, Brie. Take good steps forward. What was it you said? The stops along the way help us to the next step, or trip us up."

Brie beamed at Piper's recollection. "Yes, and when we trip, we shift our direction. There's always hope when we do. Looks like you are a hundred steps further along than last time." She glanced over her shoulder. "That's a great family to work for."

"That's my family!" Maelyn squealed.

Brie raised an eyebrow at Piper.

"Lance is Maelyn's father." She opened the car door for Maelyn, who crawled inside. Brie leaned down and waved to Maelyn before Piper shut the door.

When Piper turned around, Brie stood up with a sobered gaze. "And? Lance knew all this time?"

Piper shook her head. "Now he does. It's all good. I think it's safe to say I shifted in the wrong direction back then."

"Which has led you here, in a very different situation. A job and a roof over your head." Brie cupped her cheek.

"Is that all, though? Shouldn't the job and the roof be my own doing? I feel like I am still so dependent on others."

"There's nothing wrong with leaning into people. We're made for community. Helping each other out is the best part of life." She glanced over at the shelter. "I think so, anyway." She winked. "Your family over there thinks the same, as far as I can tell."

"Oh, not my family—" Piper hesitated, feeling like a traitor. How many times had Don and Janet, Sid... and even Lance referred to Piper as part of the family? Isn't that what she wanted all along?

Lance and Sidney carried the empty crates out and loaded them into the trailer. She winced at how hurt Sidney had seemed by Piper's choice to stay away. All because she'd kept Maelyn a secret. What choices had she made to show the Hudsons how much she cared about them like they'd obviously cared for her?

"Brie, I don't know how to be my own person *and* lean into others." Piper searched the wise woman's eyes beyond her spunky frames.

Brie held out her hand, and Piper grasped it. With a

gentle squeeze, Brie offered, "Piper, you know who you are. It's all wrapped up in Whose you are. He places people in your life to help you, or those who need your help." She squeezed her hand again. "And having folks share the journey with you for the long haul? Well, darling, that is not just happenstance. That's roots grown deep."

A wave of peace tumbled over Piper. Maybe Maelyn wasn't the only Gray who shared in those strong roots of the Hudson family. "They are my family, too. I shouldn't have said they weren't."

"What about you and Lance?" Brie gave a mischievous grin. "Any spark?"

Piper shook her head. "We are focused on Mae." She turned her attention to her daughter, ignoring the truth she'd just denied. A spark? Definitely. But Lance, Piper and Maelyn had been through enough. Falling in love with Lance Hudson was the last thing she needed to focus on, even if it was the one thing she could hardly deny anymore.

Piper tossed and turned Sunday night, waking up before the sun on Monday morning. While she put on her makeup, she received a response to her job application. She whispered a prayer of thanks. That was super quick. A solid step in the right direction.

By the time the house was flooded with the pale light of dawn, Piper was dressed in her orchard polo shirt, eating cereal and ready to send the text that had kept her up:

Sid, I am sorry for losing it on Saturday. The reason I didn't reach out back then is because I didn't want you all to wonder about Maelyn. It was foolish and unfair. To you...to Lance. I will never forgive myself for it. I felt completely stuck and on my own. Now I realize how important family is and how much I hope I can still be part of yours. I hope you can forgive me.

She paused. Lance should know this, too. She added his number, then pressed send. More steps forward. But it wasn't until she pulled into the orchard that she remembered that just because she had done her part, didn't mean that all was well.

Piper emerged from her car and crossed the parking lot to where Sidney sat waiting, on a hay bale near the entrance. Her legs were crossed, and she balanced a coffee mug on her knee.

Her sapphire eyes were unwavering as she set down the mug and stood. "I appreciate your apology." She tapped the pocket with her phone sticking out. "But there is something we need to clear up. You, Piper Elaine Gray, are not a charity case. Do you not remember how we met?"

Piper tried to breathe away the feeling that she'd been punched in the gut. This was not what she'd expected. She did remember. "I think you had spilled your juice at lunch and all the girls were laughing because it was all over your skirt."

"Yes. And they were calling me a baby. First grade, I think? Being a baby was the biggest insult." Sidney quietly chuckled. Her eyes began to fill with tears. "But you—you stuck up for me. You told them to hush, and you dug in your backpack and gave me an extra pair of shorts."

"I think I was going to have a sleepover at my granny's that weekend."

"And then, whenever you found me alone, you wouldn't just sit and be my friend. You coached me on how to stand up for myself."

Piper gasped. "That's right! You were so quiet. I think the whole school called me the Sidney whisperer at one point."

"Piper, you were the only person I would talk to. I didn't trust anyone else because of that first day with the juice."

"That was a long time ago."

"But don't you understand? You were number one to me. And you were welcomed into our house from that first playdate. Which I invited you to. Actually, my mom did."

"That was the summer before my mom married her ex." Piper sat next to her. "That was a disaster." She snaked her arm across Sid's shoulders. "Thank you for adopting me." They both laughed quietly.

Sidney patted her knee. "Now. I think you should talk to Lance."

"There really is nothing more to say. He's doing a great job with Mae."

"But what about the two of you?" Sidney sipped her coffee. "I mean, you have a kid together."

"Yep, and we will work out a schedule so he can see her all the time."

"Don't you think there's more between you and Lance than a schedule for custody?"

Piper grinned sadly. "I would never expect anything from Lance. Not after all I've put him through. Lance doesn't need—"

Lance cleared his throat. He stood at the metal building door, a debonair smile growing on his clean-shaven face. "Just like old times. You two talking about me without me around." He crossed over to them. "Sid, there's a call on hold in the office for you."

"Maybe there is, maybe there isn't," Sidney muttered

to Piper, flashing a matchmaker grin as if Lance were making an excuse to be alone with Piper.

"Ha, ha." She rolled her eyes, but all sorts of wings flurried in her belly.

Lance rocked on his heels. "Thanks for the text." His gaze was soft, skimming over her face as if he were seeing her for the first time. As if he were memorizing each freckle and eyelash.

"An apology was long overdue."

"I am sorry that you didn't feel like you could come to me in the first place." His stare was so intense, she dropped hers to his lips then quickly away.

"I am so glad Mae has you now." She stepped back on wobbly legs.

Lance hooked his hand on the back of his neck. "Thing is, Piper, I messed up, too. When you told me that you thought it was best for you to patch things up with Garrett, I just let you go. Mostly because I was going to California that week. I can't help but wonder what would have happened if I had let go of playing it safe—" He pressed his lips together, and the same sprinkle of dimples appeared on his chin as Maelyn's when she was trying to make a decision. "I—I wrote these letters, and I can't help but think about what if—"

"I never received letters from you, Lance." Her stomach dropped. What if she'd gotten letters from Lance Hudson?

"I didn't send them. Before I sent the first one, Sid told me you were engaged. The second one was—" He shifted his feet. "My response to your news." He was adorably sheepish in every way—the way he winced and shrugged and clenched his teeth in an inaudible *oops*.

Piper laughed. "Really? I wish you had sent them."

"I was like a lovesick puppy." He smirked.

"You mean, *teddy bear*?" Piper playfully punched his arm. This time, he caught it, and she let him. He held her hand to his chest. "Lance—"

"Piper, do you think we have a chance? I mean, what if Maelyn's parents were actually—together?"

Piper faced this guy she'd looked up to all her life, who'd secretly won her affection by his heroic protection and irresistible smile. Eight years had blinked by only to give her a fresh start…and a second chance? But this wasn't just about her. "We are doing what's best for Maelyn, right?"

Lance pressed his forehead to hers. "I think so."

She was so close to him, inhaling his scent, wanting desperately to close the space between them and feel her lips on his. But Piper's last relationship had been devastating to her daughter. "You are the best thing to happen to Mae, Lance. If something didn't work out… well, I can't mess things up for her. We can't."

He pulled away and grimaced, looking everywhere but in her eyes. "Yeah. I don't ever want that to happen."

"Let's be the best parents the girl could ask for. I am starting today. I have an interview after work." She smiled wide and jested, "You won't be my boss for long, Mr. Lance." She playfully punched him again. This time, he didn't catch her fist but smiled and flimsily saluted her instead.

## Chapter Twenty-One

Lance rubbed his jaw, watching Piper slip into the metal building. Had he ever felt anything close to this connection with that redhead who always seemed to disappear a little too early for Lance's preference?

Of course, he would never do anything to hurt Maelyn. If the mother of his child suggested there was any possibility of that, he chose to listen. But he wasn't completely convinced that a relationship with Piper Gray would do anything of the sort.

The most shocking thing about his breakup with Tara wasn't her affair, but her uncertainty about whether they had ever been in love. He knew himself better than Tara. He *had* fallen in love with her. Even though Lance may play it safe, he definitely didn't play a part when his heart was concerned.

Lance Hudson had fallen in love two times in his life. And neither time was out of some sort of convenience or easygoing summer fling.

Far from it.

Those unmailed letters reminded him of his very real feelings for Piper.

So, the fact that he had a daughter's heart to protect made him all the more sober to the importance of perfect timing—not in Lance convincing Piper to be together, but that she was the one person in this whole world that was the best thing to happen to him. Or at least, she was tied with their daughter.

He spent the rest of the morning finishing the pumpkin patch archway, hanging a sign that Maelyn helped paint in green letters—The Patch o' Punkins—then setting up all the tools and materials needed to finish off the gazebo steps. Two more days to work on this place before their Wednesday opening. Of course, the pumpkins were ready to pick now, but Lance couldn't help indulging Sidney's vision for a spectacular experience for every pumpkin-picking family. Lance must admit that this project wasn't just about a business plan but a fantastic way to spend time with his new daughter.

By the time Maelyn's bus arrived, Lance picked her up, and she helped him sort some crates for the next order to Clyde's. They drove the back way to the pumpkin patch since Piper had left early to get to her interview.

Lance put the truck in Park and ran around to open Maelyn's door.

"Wait!" Maelyn rummaged in her backpack. "I have something for you." She pulled out a folded piece of paper and a marker. "Here you go." She bounced in her seat, her face beaming with excitement.

Lance unfolded the page. In childlike lettering was a list:

Mr. Lance is:
 kind
 fun
 nice
 apples

Lance chuckled at that last one. But his smile froze when he read the bottom. *Dads are kind, fun, nice and maybe like apples*, then the most adorable equation, *Mr. Lance = Dad*.

"I made that in the art center," Maelyn exclaimed.

"This is the best thing I've ever seen." He folded the page up and began to place it in his pocket.

"You missed the best part!" Maelyn reached for the page. "Turn it over."

Lance unfolded the page again and looked at the back. In red ink, there was a question:

*Can I call you Dad?*

And two drawn boxes, one labeled *No* and one labeled *Yes*.

Lance's heart flipped in his chest. He smiled so wide he wondered if he should add *ridiculous* to the list.

"That's why I gave you the marker, silly." She giggled.

Lance checked the *Yes* box as if he were happily signing away his life. And really, he was—very, very happily.

"Yay!" Maelyn slid down from the truck seat, found the running board with her sneakers and wrapped her arms around Lance. Lance set down the marker and paper and lifted his little girl into the biggest hug he could muster.

She pulled back and looked at him, cupping his cheeks in her small hands. "I love you, Daddy." Her raspy voice was just like her mama's, but Lance had never heard those words from Piper.

"Oh, Maelyn, I love you, too." Lance kissed her forehead. "Thank you for being you."

And suddenly, he realized what had been missing this whole time. Not for him, or Maelyn or the apple orchard. But for the spunky redhead who'd once spun his heart as quickly as his daughter just had. Piper was everything he'd ever wanted, from that very first kiss beneath the gazebo to the moment he saw her that first day here. No matter her mistakes or his. Their biggest mistake was staying apart. She just needed to see it to believe it.

"Mae, let's go up to the house. I have something I want you to give your mom when she gets home tonight."

"Okay, Daddy." She scrambled back inside the truck, and he jogged around the truck, unable to keep from smiling—at his new name and the what-if he would finally make happen.

After arranging to take off early, Piper was thankful that Maelyn would be safe with Lance while she headed to the interview. She first talked with the preschool director, then they went to observe the classroom. She shared with the director the same thing she'd told Lance the day she'd helped the little boy write his letters on the field trip. "Helping kids is not nearly as difficult as helping adults." She added, "It's so rewarding, too."

The director agreed and talked more. For the rest of the conversation, Piper imagined Lance standing over her shoulder, whispering affirmations to Piper as a mom, an employee and any other chance he took to boost her confidence, whether he knew it or not.

Piper left the school feeling as though her greatest reference was Lance Hudson, in her own mind, anyway. Funny how she'd escaped one guy who criticized her constantly and had nearly fallen into the arms of a guy who complimented her…lifted her up.

Truthfully, she had fallen a long time ago but swept it under the carpet just like the Grays had been prone to do. But lately, Mom was softer, more willing to admit her mistakes—and it had started with the day Piper shared Maelyn's paternity and Mom acknowledged her own regrets.

As Piper drove home, she considered what life might be like if she trusted her heart to Lance. To try and make it work, like he'd suggested.

He forgave her, after all.

Piper adjusted the rearview mirror and spied Mae's locket glinting in the late afternoon sun. It must have fallen off again. When she stopped driving, she would text Lance right away so Mae wouldn't worry.

Piper pressed her hand on her own locket.

The verse inside was security that she and Mae would be together, with God by their side. *Wherever you go, I will go... Your God will be my God.*

Funny—it seemed Lance was part of this path they were taking together. She had two people with her, in good choices and bad. That was a heavy weight for one woman to bear. Did Piper really hold two people ransom to her every step?

Her phone rang, and she answered it through Bluetooth.

"Hello?"

"Hi, Piper. It's Brie. How was your interview?"

"How did you know?"

"Just got off the phone with the director. You put me down as a personal reference, remember?"

"Oh, yes. Wow. That was fast."

"Good. They sound like they like you. But I wanted to see what you thought about another opportunity here at the shelter."

"Oh, what's that?"

"I need an instructor to teach women about goal-setting and life skills. The main branch is offering free training to instructors. I can't help but think of the joy you would offer these women."

A few months ago, Piper would never have thought she'd qualify for such a position. Life skills? Uh, discouraged by Garrett. Goal-setting? Uh, food on the table was it.

But now?

Brie continued, "You know how hard it is to think beyond survival mode. And how hard it is to forgive yourself when your child is involved." Piper placed her hand on her necklace again. Walking out on Garrett was the best thing she could have done with Maelyn involved. But unease had her grip the necklace tight. "And look at you now. Two prospective jobs and a supportive family. So, what do you say? Will you think about it?"

Piper curled her hand on the steering wheel. "There's one thing, Brie. I don't know how to forgive myself. Poor Mae was born into such strife."

Brie took a beat, then responded, "I get that, Piper. But what I saw was a happy little girl surrounded by folks who love her. Looks like whatever you aren't forgiving yourself for is something that's been redeemed. Or is being redeemed…one step at a time."

"Thank you, Brie. I hope you are right. I'd hate to be blindsided by something I think is good but, in the end, burns us again."

"Trust yourself, Piper. You've come so far. I trust you for this job I'm offering. Think about it and let me know, okay?"

"Okay. Thanks again." As Piper ended the call with Brie, she focused on the horizon ahead, the old water tower painted with the Rapid Falls Eagles logo outlined by the dimming sky. She had once run away from Rapid

Falls with a secret and a misconception of what family was—and could be. But now, she raced toward it, hoping that if Lance Hudson could forgive her, like he'd said, maybe she could forgive herself, too.

# Chapter Twenty-Two

Sidney and Maelyn sat on the top step of the porch, looking at a book together.

Piper parked in the family driveway and walked over. "Hey, girls. I guess Lance is busy?" Her face heated when Sidney's eyebrow hooked with interest. "Usually Lance hangs out with Mae, that's all."

"He got a package of lighting for the gazebo that he wanted to set up before it gets dark."

Mae piped in, "Auntie Sid is showing me your yearbook."

Piper groaned and rolled her eyes. "My eyes were half shut in that picture."

Sidney slid the book from their laps and clapped it closed. "At least you weren't going through an awkward hair phase. My bangs were way too short." She stood and offered a hand to help Mae. "So, how was the interview?"

"Really good. I got another job offered to me, too." She reached out to Mae, who jumped into her arms. "At the women's shelter, actually."

"My, my, Piper-the-Great. The world is your orchard." Sidney's eyes sparkled as she grinned at her play on words. "Guess you didn't need that letter of recommendation I wrote."

"I haven't been offered the school job yet—"

"Oh, Mommy! My daddy has a letter for you. It's in my backpack." Sidney and Piper exchanged curious looks as Maelyn dug into her bag. "Here you go." She handed her an envelope with her name on it.

"Maybe he wrote a letter of recommendation, too?" Sidney shrugged. Amelia's cry emitted from the baby monitor tucked in Sidney's back pocket. "Duty calls… and I want to know what that says, Piper." She walked to the front door. "Okay?" she called.

"Okay." Piper sat down where Sidney had sat. "We'll leave in a minute, Mae."

Maelyn ran across the porch and climbed in a rocker. "Okay. I've been wanting to rock all night."

Piper giggled and pulled out folded pages. Letters, but not of recommendation—two letters dated eight years ago. Lance had kept the letters he'd written and never sent? She read the first one:

Dear Piper,
I know you've made your choice, but I don't think you know that my choice was YOU long before Garrett showed up. I used to act annoyed when you'd convince Sid to play hide-and-seek in the Vander Walt cornfield or go fishing at midnight when Mom and Dad were asleep, but what I really felt was jealous. I wanted to love life like you, and this past summer that happened because we were together. That weekend at the July Fourth celebration wasn't just a whim on my part. Have I ever had a whim? I know you are rolling your eyes right now. But that weekend happened after

I finally figured something out. Sure, all those times I followed you and Sid, I wanted to make sure my sister was not getting into trouble, but she wasn't the only one. I was checking on you, too. To make sure you were okay, and to just see you.

I guess, I wasn't jealous of your love for life. I was, and I still am, in love with you, Piper Gray. I love your joy, your funny words, your pretty smile. Now, I sit in this tiny dorm room while everyone is partying outside for homecoming. But all I can dream about is coming home to you.

I feel dumb writing this. You have Garrett. But I hope one day, you will change your mind.
Love,
Lance

Piper tried to force her tears away. Why was he sharing this with her now? And why hadn't he sent it? She picked up the next folded piece of paper with shaky fingers. It was dated about a month later.

Piper,
I heard about your engagement. Man, I should have sent you a letter before now. I had one ready to go right before Sidney told me. I'll always wonder if you'd have chosen me had I been more courageous…if I had begged you to try long-distance instead of going with Garrett.

I don't think I will send this. It's just not fair to you. I was too late. And—

The letter wasn't finished.
Piper gaped at the two letters. All this time, she'd thought she'd fallen much harder for Lance than he

could ever fall for her. She was the one who was in love with her best friend's brother much longer than she'd care to admit. And her own dream—that he was protecting her as much as Sidney each time he came after them—had been true.

There was one more page, folded separately from the other two. She unfolded it. The layout was different. Like a list. With checkboxes at the bottom.

Maelyn ran up and stood over her shoulder. "Hey, that's like the note I gave Daddy today."

"Daddy?" Piper looked up at her.

"I decided that's what he's called now." She ran her tongue over her bottom lip like she did when she was proud of herself.

Piper reached up and squeezed her hand. "And you told him in a note?"

"Yes. And he said he needed to write you one, too."

Piper's chest filled with sweet anticipation—no bitterness or hesitation. She read on.

> Piper is:
>     An amazing friend
>     A perfect mother
>     And the one who got away
>     Will you just come back to me now?
>     Piper-the-Great, please check yes.

And a little box with the word *Yes* waited for her to check it.

Piper and Maelyn arrived at the pumpkin patch as the sun melted against the horizon.

Lance climbed down a ladder on one side of the gazebo adorned with twinkle lights.

"It looks so fancy," Maelyn squealed as she and Piper walked down the path lined with sprawling pumpkin vines.

Lance met them at the entrance to the gazebo. "What do you all think?"

Maelyn ran inside the gazebo and along the railing. "It's so pretty!"

Lance grinned and patted her head when she passed him. He locked eyes with Piper.

"Quite a gazebo, Mr. Lance." Piper winked.

"A dream come true."

"Not the only one, I hope." She thought about her own dream come true—the man who stood here, activating her pulse at dangerous speeds and filling her heart with so much excitement she thought it would burst.

He cocked his head and gave her a suspecting smile.

"I hope my checking *yes* is part of yours." She handed him his note.

His smile turned into a full-on grin, and he unfolded the paper and looked at it. His face fell. "You didn't check it."

"What?"

"You didn't check it." He held the paper up.

"Oh, oops." Piper shrugged her shoulders and gave an apologetic smile. She took back the paper and tucked it in her pocket. "Well, I came back. To you. And I don't want to leave anytime soon."

He gathered her hands in his. "Really?"

Piper pulled out her locket, opened it and handed him the tiny folded strip of paper. She recited as he read it, "'Don't ask me to leave and turn back. Wherever you go, I'll go.'" She bit her lip and searched the face of this man who'd given Maelyn and Piper more than a glimpse of love—but the promise of a lifetime chock-full of it. "Maelyn and I have leaned on that scripture for so long, and I can't imagine taking one more step without you beside us—" Piper pulled his hands to her heart. "Beside me."

"That's as good as a checked box." He lowered his lips to hers, and she fluttered her eyes closed. Before he kissed her, he wrapped her in a teddy-bear embrace and whispered, "I love you, Piper-the-Great."

Maelyn flung her arms around both of their waists. "I love you both." Her parents looked down at her, and they began to laugh.

"We love you too, Mae," Piper said. Piper and Lance each placed a hand on Maelyn's shoulders. Firm and secure. Exactly what Piper wanted for her daughter. She returned her attention to Lance. "And I love your daddy, Mae. So much."

He leaned over and kissed her beneath the twinkling lights of this gazebo. Piper smiled, allowing herself to finally melt into this dream come true after taking all the right steps to get here.

# Epilogue

Maelyn stood on the end of the small dock, holding the same fishing pole that her daddy had once used. Lance beamed down at his daughter while she concentrated on the bobber on the water's surface. His little girl was growing so fast. No more lisp or braids as she neared the end of second grade.

"This is taking a while," she sighed.

"Fishing takes patience, sweetheart. Don't be too upset if—" Lance stopped speaking when he saw Piper pull up beneath the cottonwood tree. "Okay, Mae. Get ready." She began to set down her pole. A slight bounce on her toes worried Lance that she'd give it away.

"Hey, you two." Piper joined them on the dock. "Mom's house is ready to sell. Can't wait to see where they end up now that Bill's been promoted."

"Did you go back to work?" Lance tapped a white spot on her nose. "You have paint."

Piper grinned. "No, I didn't. Brie let me take the day off."

In the distance, Sidney and Todd appeared at the trailhead with Amelia in the stroller. Sidney held her phone to video what was about to happen. Lance's heart thrummed wildly. He nudged Maelyn, who was already squeezing past Piper on the dock.

"Where are you going, Mae?" Just as planned, Maelyn ran and Piper turned to watch her. "What's going on—" Piper turned back to Lance.

He pulled out the ring box from his pocket and took a knee. "Piper Elaine Gray, will you marry me?"

Piper cupped her hand over her mouth, but her typical mischievous green eyes simmered. "Where's the checkbox, Mr. Lance?"

"Always the jokester."

She bent down and flung her arms around his neck, kissing him firmly on the lips. "Always. But I am serious when I say, yes, Lance Hudson. I will happily *appley* marry you."

\* \* \* \* \*

# Get 3 FREE REWARDS!

**We'll send you 2 FREE Books plus a FREE Mystery Gift.**

**FREE** Value Over **$20**

Both the **Love Inspired®** and **Love Inspired®** Suspense series feature compelling novels filled with inspirational romance, faith, forgiveness and hope.

---

**YES!** Please send me 2 FREE novels from the Love Inspired or Love Inspired Suspense series and my FREE gift (gift is worth about $10 retail). After receiving them, if I don't wish to receive any more books, I can return the shipping statement marked "cancel." If I don't cancel, I will receive 6 brand-new Love Inspired Larger-Print books or Love Inspired Suspense Larger-Print books every month and be billed just $6.49 each in the U.S. or $6.74 each in Canada. That is a savings of at least 16% off the cover price. It's quite a bargain! Shipping and handling is just 50¢ per book in the U.S. and $1.25 per book in Canada.* I understand that accepting the 2 free books and gift places me under no obligation to buy anything. I can always return a shipment and cancel at any time by calling the number below. The free books and gift are mine to keep no matter what I decide.

Choose one:
- ☐ **Love Inspired Larger-Print** (122/322 BPA GRPA)
- ☐ **Love Inspired Suspense Larger-Print** (107/307 BPA GRPA)
- ☐ **Or Try Both!** (122/322 & 107/307 BPA GRRP)

Name (please print)

Address                                                                          Apt. #

City                                    State/Province                    Zip/Postal Code

**Email:** Please check this box ☐ if you would like to receive newsletters and promotional emails from Harlequin Enterprises ULC and its affiliates. You can unsubscribe anytime.

---

Mail to the **Harlequin Reader Service:**
**IN U.S.A.:** P.O. Box 1341, Buffalo, NY 14240-8531
**IN CANADA:** P.O. Box 603, Fort Erie, Ontario L2A 5X3

**Want to try 2 free books from another series? Call 1-800-873-8635 or visit www.ReaderService.com.**

LIRLIS23

# HARLEQUIN
## PLUS

Try the best multimedia
subscription service for romance
readers like you!

---

## Read, Watch and Play.

Experience the easiest way to get
the romance content you crave.

Start your **FREE TRIAL** at
<u>www.harlequinplus.com/freetrial</u>.